HUNGRY LIKE THE WITCH

THE WITCHES OF HOLIDAY HILLS COZY MYSTERIES

CAROLYN RIDDER ASPENSON

W itches and other supernaturals work. We have human jobs. We have bills to pay, apartments to rent, doctors to visit. Everything a human requires to survive, we require as well. My job was my dream job, and I was blessed to have it. I write books. Cozy mysteries with a splash of magic. Since my mother passed and her spell over me died with her, my witchy cozies could be considered non-fiction in a sense because I don't just write about witches. I am one.

"I had the eeriest dream last night." I set my pink and black backpack and black purse on the table and twisted my curly hair into a ball, then clipped it on top of my head. It had grown like a weed over the past year, spreading my curls dangling down to my waist.

"Your collar," my best friend Stella said. "It's tucked under on the right."

I fixed it and plopped into my chair beside her. "Anyway, so I'm here, at the Enchanted Café, working on my book, and this guy walks in."

"Was he cute?"

"No, but I expected you to ask. He dressed like he lived in a mountain cabin with no running water. His beard hung to his chest." I shuddered. "It was disgusting. There was dirt and food stuck in it."

"That's gross."

"Trust me, you have no idea. Oh, and his mane was just as nasty."

"His mane?" She angled her head to the side. "Have you been reading the thesaurus before you fall asleep again?"

"It improves my writing."

She rolled her eyes. "I guess."

"Anyway, so his *tresses* had gnarly knots everywhere."

She crossed her arms. "The editor in me is screaming right now."

"Sorry about that. The worst thing about the dream was his smell. Body odor, dirt, feces, all these foul scents blending into one revolting stench."

She held up a finger. "Hold on. You smell in your dreams?"

I nodded. "Don't you?"

"Uh, no. Do you dream in color too?"

"You don't?" I asked.

She shook her head. "Wow. I thought my subconscious would be a lot more exciting than yours."

"Just wait. It gets weirder. He wore a clown nose. You know, those huge, red bulbs you see on clowns in horror movies?" I shivered. "Freaked me out."

She grimaced. "I hate clowns."

"So do I! My mom took me to a carnival in Alpharetta when I was five. They had a fun house, and she forced me to go into it."

"That's awful."

"You have no idea. The place was full of creepy clowns

with big red noses and lips, dark circles around their eyes, and those gigantic, curly, bright colored wigs. I shrieked when they stomped their clown feet."

"I'm sweating just from hearing that."

"Sorry. At least this one wasn't like that. He wasn't a real clown, though. He just had on the nose. Anyway, he walked over to me and said, *Gabe's not coming home.*"

She set down her pumpkin spice latte as her eyes widened. "Okay, that is awful. What happened next?"

"I asked him who he was and what he knew."

"And?"

"And nothing. He just flipped around and walked out." For a moment, the dream latched onto me again, the man's cold, dark eyes penetrating my soul. I shivered. "It felt so real. Every detail." I glimpsed around the Enchanted. "And the Enchanted? It's like I was there in real time. It all matched." I pointed to the front table. "Even Bessie's book of the month choice."

Stella scooted her chair away from the table and crossed one leg over the other. Her outfit matched her personality. Tight, black, skinny jeans with a black and silver v-neck sweater, and a pair of black boots. She left her long hair down, straightened and slicked with a shiny gloss. Her silver hoop earrings hung through her hair almost to her neck. "You're right. That is weird, but it's only a dream. Don't let it bother you."

"I'm trying, but sometimes they linger throughout the day." I removed a file folder from my backpack and set it on the table. "But it can't today. Besides working on my manuscript, I've got to review the plans for the Fall Mum Festival. There's a planning meeting tonight, and I need to get my notes in order. Now that the rain stopped, I think we can set up."

"You mean the monsoon? I ruined a pair of leather boots running home last night."

"Running home from where?"

"I stopped at the candy shop down the street. Okay, I didn't stop there. I went there during that break in the rain. My weather app said it wouldn't start up for another hour, but it was wrong. I took the shortcut and ran through the back alley by the church. It's a muddy mess over there. My boots sank into it. They're ruined."

"That's awful."

"The boots cost me a hundred bucks. So, you're going to the meeting?"

Stella knew I despised the meetings. Some of the members disagreed on everything from the color of the posters to the type of popcorn purchased. Those who didn't get along made effective planning almost impossible. I stuck it out because of my mother. She'd created the festival fifteen years before, and when she was sick, I promised her I'd make sure it continued. I couldn't go back on my word. The festival had meant the world to her and keeping it running kept a part of her alive. I just wished the committee members didn't act like preschoolers fighting for a box of crayons.

Mr. Charming, a green and yellow parrot with excellent hearing and repetition skills, sat on his perch on top of the front counter. Mr. Hastings, an older warlock who'd been coming to the Enchanted since I was a kid, walked in. He meandered over to the counter and bellowed out his regular order, a coffee with cream. He offered no greeting, no smile, nothing. Typical for the cranky warlock. Bessie Frone, the owner, and my deceased mother's best friend smiled regardless. Bessie didn't get upset easily, but when she did, people ran for cover. Her magical abilities broke records.

"And don't put any of that special stuff in it this time. I've got a doctor's appointment today. I don't need anything showing up in my blood work," Mr. Hastings said.

Bessie smiled. "Sure thing, Waylon. Let me get that for you."

Stella pivoted in her chair to watch the show we both knew was coming. Mr. Charming, once my mother's familiar who, after her death, switched to protecting Bessie, liked to poke the bear, and especially with those who hadn't fallen for his charms. He bobbed back and forth for Mr. Hastings's attention, but the elderly warlock ignored him. Theirs was a love hate relationship. Mr. Charming loved Mr. Hastings, but those feelings fell flat. Mr. Charming sat on Mr. Hastings' last nerve every time he came in. I knew one day that nerve would rip, and goddess only knew what would happen.

"Mr. Charming loves coffee," he said. "Coffee with the good stuff. The cantankerous old coot."

Stella's hand shot to her mouth, but not in time to cover her burst of laughter. She gasped when Mr. Hastings swiveled toward her and glared into and through her soul with his dark eyes. "Oh, I'm sorry," she said. She flipped back toward me with her eyes widened. "Whoops."

I giggled. "Bessie must stop referring to her customers with descriptive words."

Cooper, my Burmese cat and familiar, pawed at my leg. I bent down and smiled at him. "Yes, Coop?"

He licked his lips. "If you're trying to starve me to death, it's working." He tipped to his side and fell over. His bulky, brick-like muscles making a thud sound on the floor. "I won't make it much longer."

Stella gazed at him, then raised an eyebrow at me. "I swear sometimes that cat thinks he's talking to you."

If she only knew. Stella's human ears heard only Cooper's meows. My witch ears heard it all. His babbling. His food-loving moans, his snoring, his meowing. He'd blessed me with all the sounds. Twenty-four-seven. I didn't mind most of them, but the food-loving moans? I cringed at those. Sometimes they bordered on obscene. "He is. He's hungry."

She tilted her head and studied him, then sat straight in her chair. "I think he could skip a meal and be just fine."

I glimpsed Coop's eyes grow wide as he said, "Did she just call me fat?"

I bit my bottom lip. "Let me get him his tuna, otherwise he'll never stop talking." I walked behind the counter and into the kitchen.

Bessie leaned against a large steel sink. "Is it safe to go out there?"

"You heard Mr. Charming?"

"Calling Waylon Hastings a cantankerous old coot?" She nodded. "I need to stop giving my customers nicknames."

"Might be a wise decision."

She poured a shot of cream into Mr. Hastings's cup, then sprinkled a dash of something that turned the coffee pink for a moment. Little sparks floated into the air. "Perfect!"

I examined the inside of the cup and waited for something else to happen. "What did you put in there today?"

"It's a new mix I'm trying. Turmeric, snail shell, white oak bark, and a hint of my secret ingredient."

"Sounds crunchy." I reached for the cup. "I'll give it to him. Maybe I can turn his frown upside down."

"If you can't, that coffee will." She winked.

"Um? Hello?" Cooper said below me. He hopped onto the counter and pawed at Bessie. "The witch is forcing me to diet. I'm withering away to nothing here. I need tuna, stat."

Bessie rubbed Cooper's ears and gave me a stern warning. "If you keep trying to starve this sweet boy, I'm going to steal him away from you."

Cooper pushed the side of his face into her palm. "This woman, she gets me."

"Oh, for the love of Goddess," I said. "He is not starving. Look at that belly."

Cooper sat on his back legs and examined his belly, touching it with his front paws. "What belly? That's a six pack right there, and I'm going to lose it if you don't feed me."

Bessie's lip twitched. For reasons I didn't understand, the powers that be had let Bessie hear Cooper's human-like voice. "I'll feed him. You tame the beast out in the café."

I saluted her and then pranced out of the kitchen with a smile plastered onto my face. I skipped over to Waylon Hastings and set his coffee on the small table in front of the fireplace. "Here you go, Mr. Hastings. I made sure it's just the way you like it."

He scrutinized the coffee, picking it up and swirling it in the cup as if he could see the special ingredients in the liquid. He glanced up at me. "She didn't put any magical stuff in it, did she?"

"Nope." I crossed my heart. "Promise."

He sipped the drink then once again leaned back in his cushy leather chair and smiled. "Thanks for taking care of me, Abby. That ancient witch in there likes to drop a little magic in my coffee now and then. She says it lightens my mood."

Mr. Charming flew over and perched on the back of Mr. Hastings's chair. "The good stuff. He gets the good stuff. Cantankerous old coot."

I grimaced, then I pressed my lips together and tilted my head to the side. "He watches a lot of TV."

The front entrance door swung open, and Mr. Calloway, one of Holiday Hills' more popular shape shifters, stepped inside.

"Saved by the bell," I mumbled. "Good morning, Mr. Calloway. How are you?"

He removed his top hat, something he had taken to wearing often due to his growing receding hairline. He placed the top hat on the floor next to his regular chair and sighed as he guided his older bones to sit. "It's getting rough, Abby, being an old man, I mean. Last night I was out wandering through town, and that old witch off Mayberry Street? You know the one I'm talking about, right?"

"Isabelle Ryland?" Isabelle wasn't ancient, at least not as old as Mr. Calloway. If I remembered right, she'd been born in the 1800s, making her a toddler in witch years. Me? I was a newborn.

He nodded. "She was out at her mailbox, and when she saw me, she thought I was a coyote. A coyote!" He shook his head. "I've been a scary looking wolf since the 1700s, and that woman called me a coyote."

Mr. Hastings guffawed. "You know you can fix that." He flipped his head toward the kitchen. "I bet Bessie can whip up something that will grow that hair back. Maybe even a little of the muscle tone, too."

Stella wandered over. We nixed the magic talk. "Good morning, gentlemen," she said. She flashed them a big smile, highlighting her pearly white teeth.

They returned the gesture but didn't speak. Stella had a way of taming the beast in men of any age. For humans, it was her pheromones. They eluded a Marilyn Monroe-esque, innocent sexiness that threw every man for a loop. My pheromones turned men into frogs. For magicals, like Mr. Hastings and Mr. Calloway, well, let's just say Stella brought the human out in them as well. My track record with magical men wouldn't have won me any awards. I'd only dated one, and he'd disappeared on a mission for the MBI, the Magical Bureau of Investigations, several months back. I hadn't heard from him in four months.

Stella waited for them to say something, but they sat there, staring at their feet like middle school boys. She eyed me, and I shrugged. She rolled her eyes, then flipped around and sauntered back to our table. The two men watched her.

I hitched my left hip out, then placed my fist on it, shaking my head at them. "You know it's not good manners to gawk at a woman behind her back. And ignoring her? I expect more from you two. You've been around too long to treat a lady like that."

They both dipped their chins to their chest and groaned. "She's right," Mr. Calloway said.

"We'll be better next time."

I eyed Mr. Hastings. He shrunk lower in his seat. "She's just so pretty. It ties my tongue up in knots just to look at her."

I chuckled. "I can see how that would be true." I shifted toward Mr. Callaway. "Would you like your regular drink this morning?"

He smiled up at me. "Yes, please, and ask Bessie if she has something she can add for hair loss and depleted muscle tone while you're at it." He shot Mr. Hastings a snarl. "If she does, give him a refill with it, too."

Hastings chuckled. "Can't argue with that."

"I'll get that for you," I said. As I stepped away, I swirled around and pointed at the men, then pointed at my eyes, and back at them again, mouthing, "I'm watching you," as I did.

Mr. Charming flapped his green wings and said, "Hair loss and depleted muscle. Hair loss and depleted muscle. Cantankerous old coot. Cantankerous old coot."

Back in the kitchen, Cooper lay on his back on the counter, a definite health code violation. He groaned as Bessie scratched his belly. Burmese cats weren't like regular cats. Magical being aside, Burmese were personable and playful. They loved attention, required lots of snuggles, and didn't bat an eye at a belly rub. Their downside? They had no personal space, and they snored. At least Cooper did.

Prior to my mother's passing and the binding spell she'd placed over my powers dying along with her, Cooper had been just a cat in my eyes. We snuggled. He would lie on my chest and breathe his tuna breath into my face as I slept. We were inseparable best friends. He was there for me through my divorce, the worst time of my life, and when my mother died. The inseparable best friends' part hadn't changed, but when a cat lay on my chest babbling on about tuna? Boundaries mattered. My chest was off limits.

I stomped my foot. "Are you kidding me? He just chowed down a whole can of tuna in what? Three minutes? And now you're helping him slide into a food coma? What if a demon warlock with a red clown nose comes rushing in here to kill me? His little comatose self would be useless."

He rolled over onto his tummy, then stretched into the downward cat pose and then reverse downward cat. I thought he would have stood and defended himself, but nope. He ended up lying back down for a snooze. I glanced over at Bessie, whose wide eyes and raised eyebrows made me laugh.

"It was a smaller can than normal." She tilted her head. "Why would you think a demon warlock with a red clown nose would come in here and try to kill you? Is something going on?"

I jumped up onto the counter and sat next to my cat. I stroked my hand down his silky, brown fur. "I don't and no. Nothing's going on. I just had this weird dream some mountain man with a red clown nose came in here and told me that Gabe wasn't coming back."

"Why did you call it a demon warlock?"

"I don't know. I just said that because he was so creepy. I don't know if he wanted to kill me. It was just a message. I'm sure it's just my subconscious dealing with the fact that Gabe has been missing in action in my life for months now." Before Bessie could say anything else, I said, "Mr. Calloway would like his regular with a splash of hair growth and muscle, if you've got it."

Bessie shifted toward her shelf of special ingredients and fished through the bottom shelf. "Oh, I think I have the perfect spell for his problems."

"Great. I'll let him know you'll have it out in a minute."

I walked out of the kitchen to Constance Ambrosia, another committee member standing at the counter. "Hey Constance. Bessie's in the kitchen. Can I get you something?"

She fluttered her eyelashes. I would have died for those. So thick, and dark, and without mascara. "Good morning, Abby. What a joy it is to see you. Yes. I would love an Earl Grey tea, please."

"I'll get that started for you." Her feet barely touched the ground as she swept across the floor. She sat at a table near the opposite wall of the fireplace in front of a large bookcase stuffed with books.

Constance carried herself with the grace of a gazelle. Everything about her said elegance. Her golden blond locks cascading down her back, her creamy white skin, and her full lips enchanted men even more than Stella. All of Holiday Hills adored her. They couldn't help themselves. Constance was an enchantress. Her magic and beauty attracted people.

I headed back into the kitchen to prepare her tea and stopped short. Cooper moaned as he snarfed down a fresh can of tuna. I peered at Bessie. "Is that another can of tuna?"

She sprinkled a powder over a cup of coffee. "He claimed he was starving."

I slid the can out from under Cooper's face. "That's enough."

He stuck out his left paw, attached it to the top of the can, and dragged it back. "I'm almost finished."

"This never ends up good, and you know it."

Bessie apologized and swore she wouldn't do it again. Cooper ignored me, even though I meant that for him.

After I finished preparing the tea, I put it on the tray with Mr. Calloway's coffee. "I'll take care of it, then I have to get to work. I have a call with my agent next week, maybe sooner, and I need to polish my manuscripts and send them to her beforehand."

"Of course, honey," Bessie said. "I thought maybe—"

A ruckus in the café interrupted her. Two loud, booming male voices screamed inappropriate words. Not cool in Bessie's café.

2

Cooper flew a foot in the air, aimed his body to the ground, dropped onto all fours, and rushed into the café, yelling, "I'm on it."

"I've got this," I said to Bessie. "You get this tray out." I raced out behind him to find Benedict Carrington, a middle-aged man and a shape shifting wolf, nose to nose with Cornelius Stone, also a middle-aged man and a warlock. Each stood almost as tall as me, at close to six feet. They'd both balled their fists so hard, their knuckles turned white. Cornelius's hand appeared even whiter from the intensity of his silver ring with the shiny black stone.

Benedict Carrington snarled at Cornelius Stone. His sharp canine teeth sparkled even in the dim light of the Enchanted. "You changed the votes. I know you did!"

"I did no such thing! The committee voted, and you lost. If you have a problem with that, take it up with Abby Odell, not me."

Cooper slid between the men, rubbing his body along each of their legs. They glanced down. The pause gave me the opportunity to jump in between them. "Take what exactly up with Abby Odell?"

Cornelius Stone stepped back. He adjusted his jacket and ran a hand through his black pompadour. "Mr. Carrington is upset the committee head job went to me. He thinks I cheated to get it."

Stella scurried by as she made her way to Mr. Hastings and Mr. Calloway. She plopped into an empty chair between them, her eyes glued just like theirs to the battle. I spied Constance watching from her table as well.

I moved to the side so I could speak to both men without having to rotate in a circle to address one or the other. "Benedict, the committee voted. I saw the votes. Cornelius won fair and square. You'll have a chance next year."

Benedict huffed. His large chest swelled, then deflated. "The spot was mine. I spoke with every committee member. They assured me they didn't want Stone as the head. You know how he is."

Just then Isaac Rivers, a warlock and committee member, strutted into the café carrying a yellow mum plant in a plastic container. Standing next to Isaac made me uncomfortable. I towered over him. I wasn't sure, but I thought it made him uneasy as well. He raised his hand and waved his long fingers with razor sharp nails. "Howdy, y'all." He stopped in his tracks, his fingers still extended in their wave. "Did I interrupt something?"

Bessie tiptoed over to Mr. Calloway and handed him his coffee. "I added a little something extra," she whispered. Then she hurried to the opposite side of the café to drop off Constance's tea. "Here you go, honey. You need anything else. Just give me a holler." She eyed the men. "Sorry about them."

I focused on the men, stepping close to them to prepare for the physical confrontation I hoped wouldn't happen.

"Isaac," Benedict said. "Perfect timing. You know Stone cheated to get the committee head position. So, go on. Tell us who you voted for."

He tweaked his neck back and swallowed. "I—"

I jumped in front of Isaac and held up my hand. "Let's not, okay?" I shook my head and groaned. "Thank you." I whipped back around to the other two. "Gentlemen, enough. Please. Now isn't the time for this discussion, and Bessie's café isn't the place."

"It's a bookshop," Cornelius said.

"See? He's always got to be starting something," Benedict said. "Always looking for an argument."

"I didn't start this one," Cornelius said. "You did."

"Gentleman," I repeated. "I said enough. Don't make me do something you'll regret." I smiled at Cornelius. "And it's a café *and* bookshop."

"It's always been a bookshop with coffee and treats," he said. "While Ms. Frone may have recently built the kitchen and expanded the menu, it's still a bookshop." He lifted his nose to me. "I see you inherited your mother's stubbornness."

"He did not say that," Cooper said. "I'll handle this."

I glanced down at my cat, hoping he could read my mind, telling him to stay out of it. Kindness and Cornelius Stone didn't jive. Everyone in Holiday Hills knew that. Most of the time, no one bothered with him, but every so often, he pulled someone's chain hard enough to force them into a fight. I thought he enjoyed it, maybe even thrived on it. I wouldn't let him do that with me.

Cooper sauntered back to Cornelius's legs and twisted through them, rubbing his scent across his pants.

Cornelius lifted his left foot and aimed his shiny black shoe at Coop.

Oh, no. I would not let him kick my cat. I glared at him and tapped my fingertip to my nose. His left foot went up higher than he'd planned, setting him off balance. He bent at the waist, threw his arms up in the air, and fell backwards. His bum hit the floor first. His head smacked the cement and bounced back up a second later.

He lay there for a moment with his eyes opened wide, then twisted his head to me and snarled. "Did you just do that?"

I pressed my palm against my chest. "Who me? Of course not. I'm all the way over here." I stretched my legs in two wide steps and crouched down next to him. "Are you okay?"

He sighed. "I think so."

Cooper climbed on top of Cornelius and sniffed his tweed blazer. His legs shook. "Oh, boy," he said. "I don't feel good." He glanced at me. "Too much tuna, too fast." He yacked like cats did before they threw up and released the tuna he'd eaten tuna right on top of Cornelius Stone's tweed blazer.

Stella's laughter filled the room. She caught herself and rushed over with a cloth from behind the counter.

I ripped Cooper from Cornelius's chest and set him on the floor. "Cooper Odell!"

Stella examined Cornelius's jacket and blanched. She lifted her hands to her ears, dropped the cloth, and said, "Nope. I'm sorry. I can't handle that."

Mr. Charming chanted from across the room. "Cooper threw up! Cooper threw up!"

I crouched down and covered the regurgitated tuna with the cloth.

Cornelius swatted at my hand, pushed himself up, and sniped, "Stop that, witch!"

I yanked the cloth off his jacket as he leaned toward me and shook the tuna from his jacket onto the floor. Cooper sauntered over to it.

"Cooper!" I hollered. "Do not!"

He gazed up at me. "But it's tuna."

I glared at him, and he retreated.

"Coopie doopie doo!" Mr. Charming said. "Coopie doopie doo!"

Cornelius's face reddened. "I'm reporting this to the Health Department. Animals shouldn't be inside eating establishments!"

Benedict crossed his arms over his chest and sneered. "Didn't you say this is a bookshop?"

Cornelius muttered many unkind things as he slammed out of the café. Bessie trailed behind him.

"I think I'd better get going," Benedict said.

"I understand," I said. "See you at the meeting later today?"

"I'll be there." He waved to Constance as he left.

Mr. Jennings and Mr. Calloway had watched him leave but returned to their conversation as if the event had never happened. I soaked some paper towels in water and cleaned up Cooper's mess while he sat and watched.

"Why don't you just use magic?" he asked.

"Personal gain. I try to keep it to a minimum. You know the powers that be aren't fans of magic being used for personal gain."

He scraped his front paw across his face. "Doesn't seem like personal gain to me. I say do it."

I glanced over at Stella. She'd set up her laptop and

tapped away on the keyboard. "Fine," I said. "But if I get in trouble for this, I'm blaming you."

"Wouldn't be the first time," he said, and skirted away.

I finished with Cooper's mess and dropped into my chair.

"Wow," Stella said. She raised both eyebrows. "Things are just pumping right into action with your committee, aren't they?"

"I don't know how my mother put up with these people. They've been on this committee for fifteen years, and most of them can't stand each other. Why they keep coming back makes no sense."

"Some people like the torture. They thrive on being annoyed and hating others." She flicked her chin toward Constance Ambrosia. "But not those two. Look at how comfy they look."

I pivoted in my chair and noticed Isaac Rivers sitting with Constance. "Oh, no. It's not what you think. Constance and Cornelius are together. I've no clue why, but they've been an item for over a year now. You know that."

She tapped a pencil on the table. "You should pay better attention to your committee members. They ended things a week ago."

"What? No. I hadn't heard. She must be so upset."

"I would be relieved. Cornelius is an arrogant snob. He's proven that time and time again. She deserves better." She pointed to my laptop. "I didn't expect you'd know. You've been head down in that manuscript for a month now, you've paid attention to nothing else."

I couldn't argue. "Manuscripts, and they're due to my agent soon. I need to polish them."

She tilted her head to the side. "I know you're concerned with book sales being down and all, but you've only written one book in your name. You know how this industry works. You need at least four books to get noticed."

"Which is why I'm submitting these next three together. I'd prefer a publisher over being self-published. There's too much work for one person when you publish on your own."

"But the money's better if you're self-published."

"I know. It's just a lot of work I didn't expect. Marketing, formatting, dealing with covers. Being on social media? Who has time for that? I've got to focus on the quality of my stories and my ability to keep my readers guessing. That takes a lot of time and effort."

Stella didn't mince words. She shot straight, even when her verbal bullets pierced my heart. "Is it really that? Or are you working so hard to forget about Gabe?"

My stomach knotted. Gabe. Gabe Ryder, the chief of police for Holiday Hills, warlock, investigator for the Magical Bureau of Investigations, and my significant other. All things amazing in my heart. Did I need the reminder that he'd gone dark on me? I'd already spent most of my free time thinking about him. Before he left, he promised he'd always be there for me. Ironic, right? "I'm not trying to forget Gabe. It's just a struggle not to talk to him."

Stella's cell phone rang. She checked the caller ID. "Oh, I need to take this." She stood and walked outside.

My stomach relaxed. I'd dodged that bullet. Talking about Gabe pained me so much my body reacted. My heart raced, and my lungs fought for air. Sometimes just thinking of him sent me slamming into an anxiety attack. I had books to polish. I refused to spend my time in the throes of anxiety attacks, so I decided to block Gabe from my mind. And I'd done that until Stella said his name. For at least an hour. Give or take.

I gathered my things and stuffed them into my bag.

Polishing manuscripts required patience and focus, and I couldn't focus inside the café then. Cooper had been snoring by my feet. I rubbed his teeny, black nose with my finger.

He opened his right eye. "Unless you're dying or bleeding, let me sleep. I'm in the middle of a glorious tuna coma here."

"I'm going back to our apartment. You coming or staying?"

He closed his eye and snored.

"All right then."

I said goodbye to the regulars, then made a quick stop to visit with Constance and Isaac. They whispered close to each other but sat up and put distance between them when they noticed me. "Hey, Constance. I heard about you and Cornelius. I'm so sorry. Are you okay?"

Her bottom lip quivered for a moment, but she wiggled her head back and forth and lifted her chin. "I'm fine. I'd had enough of Cornelius and his elitist behaviors. It was time to cut the cord."

"Do you think you'll be okay working together on the committee?"

She exhaled. "I've given it some thought, and yes. I do. I can't guarantee Cornelius won't cause problems, but I'll do my best to keep things running smoothly. I know this festival is important to you and to your mother's memory. I don't want to cause problems."

"Oh, I didn't think you would cause any problems. I'm just worried about you."

"Don't be." She waved her hand as if to dismiss my concern. "I'm fine. It was time to kick that warlock out the door."

Isaac chuckled. "Amen. I'd like to say, I think Benedict would be a better fit as the committee head."

"But didn't you vote for Cornelius?" I asked.

His long brown hair fell over his eyes. He flipped it back and dug his hand into his pocket. A second later, he'd twisted his hair into a bun on the back of his head. "Regretfully, I did. I thought of it as extending an olive branch, but I have regrets about it now. Cornelius doesn't rank high on the popularity scale, and I'm worried it might affect the festival." He smiled and pointed to his mum next to him on the floor. "Speaking of the festival, I've been working on a new fertilizer for my entry. It's coming along well. I expect it to be ready and in my plants for the competition." He leaned down to his mum plant and picked it up. "Look how great this looks."

Constance waved her hand over her face. "Ew. It stinks. Put it down."

"That's great," I said. "May we speak confidentially?"

Constance smiled. "Of course."

Isaac had picked up the mum to examine the soil. He stuck his face into the flowers then set it back on the floor. "Sure. Sounds serious. Is this about the festival?"

How do you think Deanna and Damien feel having Cornelius as the committee head?"

"Deanna had to vote for him," Constance said. She rolled her eyes. "That was the only way she'd get her little *pin the broom on the witch* game approved."

"No one else wants it?"

"You're a witch. Do you enjoy when someone mocks you?" she asked.

"I see your point," I said.

"As for Damien," she said. She held up her hand and closed her eyes while shaking her head. "I can't say. I stay clear of him. He smells so bad. I don't know what that is, but it's awful."

"You should come to more meetings," Isaac said. "See for yourself how things go."

He was right. The meetings mattered, and I should have attended more.

* * *

I spent most of the day digging into my manuscripts, over analyzing every scene, removing sentences, adding sentences, changing red herrings — all the things I did with every manuscript.

"Hey. Hey, Ab, wake up."

I opened my eyes to Cooper's paw pressed onto my nose. "I'm up." I sat up on my couch and rubbed my eyes. "I must have fallen asleep. When did you get back? What time is it?"

"I got back two hours ago. You were out like a light. It's almost nine o'clock."

"What?" I jumped from the couch. "Oh no! I missed the meeting. I needed to be there. Why didn't you wake me?"

He perched on the top of the couch. "I'm your familiar, not an alarm clock. Besides, I hadn't finished sleeping when I left the Enchanted, so I came back and napped some more. I only woke up a few minutes ago." He yawned. "I'm still tired."

I'd once read cats slept eighteen hours a day. Cooper had topped that on several days. I ambled to my bathroom as the groggy cloud of sleep lingered. After brushing my teeth, I threw on a fresh pair of clothes, and pulled my hair into a ponytail. If I was lucky, the meeting had run longer than expected, and I could catch the end.

Cooper hadn't budged from the couch. He raised his head from the cushion and bent his head to the left and then the right. "Ah. Much better. Where're you going?"

"To the church to see if anyone's still there."

"But it's past my dinner time."

I eyed his middle. "Your tummy okay?"

"My starvation is creating sharp pains in it and my intestines. I need food."

"That's not hunger. That's gas. But fine." I didn't have time to argue. I twirled my hand and an open can of tuna appeared on my coffee table. "There."

"Now that's what I call personal gain." He jumped down onto the couch seat and stretched his stout body to the can.

I draped my purse over my shoulder. My powers had expanded a while back. Not only could I make things happen, but I could also send myself places and even astral project. Projecting gave me a migraine, so I rarely did it. Both sent rushes of heat and cold through my body, and sometimes I landed in the wrong place when transporting, but practice made perfect, so I gave transporting a shot. "If you get sick, please don't do it on my new carpet."

He ignored me. "I'll come if you call."

* * *

My feet hit the ground hard. I lost my balance, swaying left, then right. I opened my eyes expecting to see the church's chapel pews or altar, but I stared into the ice cream freezer at the grocery store.

My mouth watered. Ice cream sounded delicious, but it would have to wait. I closed my eyes again, and seconds later I appeared in a small, dark alley. "Where am I?"

Crash!

I fell backwards. My purse fell from my shoulder as my back banged against something hard. I glimpsed someone or something zip by my side and behind whatever I'd hit, but it was too dark to say who or what. Had it been on all fours or just a person who'd lost their balance? I wasn't sure.

A moment passed, and my eyes still hadn't adjusted to the darkness. A rancid smell, like rotting eggs, wafted past me. I blanched and crouched down feeling for my purse. My cell phone's flashlight would provide enough light to figure out where I was.

Only I didn't grab my purse.

I grabbed a hand instead. A hand with a large ring on a finger. I gasped, fell backward, missing the hard thing I'd hit before, and patted my hand behind me for my purse. I pulled out my cell phone and hit my flashlight.

"Oh, no!" Cornelius Stone lay in front of me with a pair of pruning scissors stuck into his chest. I checked for a pulse, but he was gone.

3

Holiday Hill's Deputy Chief Harrison Martensen wobbled over, the brim of his hat pulled low over his forehead. He chewed on a piece of straw and then spit it to the ground while glowering at me. "Miss Odell." He dug into his jacket pocket and pulled out a pack of gum. He unwrapped a piece and popped it into his mouth. "Imagine my surprise, getting a call about a murder and you on scene."

Deputy Chief Martensen and I didn't mesh. If someone asked him who he considered the biggest nuisance in town, he'd pick me. One hundred percent. He disapproved of my meddling, as he'd put it, into police investigations. I disapproved of his rudeness and know-it-all impression of himself. He wasn't a know it all. He didn't know much in my book. "Deputy Martensen, I don't go looking for these things."

He blew a bubble. "So you've said. Yet here we are."

I crossed my arms over my chest and leaned against the church's brick exterior. "In case you're wondering, I've touched nothing."

He pursed his lips before speaking. "Care to explain why you and a deceased Cornelius Stone are in the back alley of the Holiday Hills Community Church at this time of night?"

Martensen was human, so telling him I'd mistakenly transported myself there instead of inside the church would have gotten me a psychological evaluation. "I fell asleep and missed the festival committee meeting. I rushed over and found Cornelius like this, then called 911."

"Did you see anyone?"

"I heard something fall, and I think I might have seen someone, but it was dark. I didn't have these enormous lights you've set up out here. So I can't be sure if it was a person or an animal."

"You can't tell the difference between an animal and a human?"

I smiled. "How similar they can look might surprise you."

He furrowed his brow. "Good to know. Now you just stay put, missy. I'll deal with you later."

Missy? Stay put? Those words weren't in my vocabulary. I snuck around the back of the trash dumpster to see what they'd blocked off with yellow police tape. The officer who had arrived first had covered Cornelius with a white sheet and blocked off a small area around his body. It didn't include the muddy section across the small alleyway. I'd have a better view of the happenings from there.

There was more mud than I'd thought. So much mud. No wonder Stella ruined her boots. I stopped at the muddy edge of the gravel path and scrutinized the area, finding what I assumed were Stella's tiny footed boot prints. The rain had almost washed them completely away.

I pivoted back toward the church to make sure Martensen didn't have eyes on me. Assured he didn't, I followed the edge of the path toward the far end of the church, but I saw nothing, so, I flipped around and went the other way. I kept going past the end of the church to see if I could locate anything related to Cornelius Stone's death.

And I did find something. Two fresh, large shoe prints shaped like sneakers. Only two. As if someone stuck their feet into the mud and pulled them back out. Except these prints resembled mud molds, undisturbed, unlike I'd have expected them to be if a person yanked their shoes out of the mud. Why would someone step into the mud and then step out? And the prints hadn't been affected by the rain. Were they new?

I studied the surrounding gravel. Though we'd had so much rain, the gravel served as a dam, blocking the mud from rising over it. If someone had walked on it with muddy shoes, there should have been muddy prints or at least remnants of mud on the rocks, but there wasn't. I rushed back to the prints I thought belonged to Stella. A small trail of decreasing mud crossed the gravel from those prints.

The only way the other prints wouldn't leave mud on the gravel or more prints in the mud was if they were from a magical.

A magical desperate to get away from a murder they'd just committed.

* * *

A growing crowd filled the Enchanted. Half the town had shown up to gossip about Cornelius Stone's murder. Bessie called in two part timers to serve coffee and pastries, yet she continued darting in and out of the group carrying trays herself. I offered to help, but she refused.

"You found Cornelius, and you're running the festival. You need to handle this," she said.

"Yes, ma'am."

I skirted past a small group of witches that liked to spread gossip. One grabbed my arm, but I yanked it away. "I've got to help Bessie," I lied. I pushed and shoved my way back to my table where Mr. Charming and Cooper sat next to my computer. Stella guarded my seat.

"Geez," she said. "This is crazy. If no one liked Stone, why are they all here?"

I leaned in close and whispered, "They don't want to miss the action, and they love a good story, especially when it's a murder."

Her eyes widened. "Murdered? Really? Do you think that? The police haven't said anything yet. What did you see?"

"I know someone murdered him. Someone stabbed him in the chest with pruning sheers. Deep into his chest." I glanced around us to make sure no one heard me. "And I think the murderer was there when I got there, but they ran." Or magically disappeared, but I couldn't say that to Stella.

She gasped. "Wait a minute. You think you saw the killer?"

"Shh." I scanned the area one more time. No one heard, but just in case, I cast a protective invisible barrier around us. "I don't want this getting around. You know how Martensen gets."

"Right. Okay." She lowered her voice. "And can you explain why you were in that alley at night?"

"I slept through the committee meeting, so I rushed over to the church to see if it was still going on."

"And you went in through the back instead of the front entrance?"

"No. I thought I heard something out back, so I went to look."

"Maybe that's what Cornelius did too. Look what happened to him. Abby, please, you must stop being so inquisitive. If not for yourself, for those that love you." She rubbed behind Cooper's ears. "And for Coopie."

"Coopie doopie do," Mr. Charming said.

"That's a nice way to say nosy."

She laughed. "It is."

"Listen, I didn't tell Martensen this, but I saw an odd set of footprints."

She raised an eyebrow. "Do you think they belonged to the murderer?"

"They were fresh. The mud's still wet enough to make prints, but not wet enough to erase them. I saw yours as well."

She sighed. "Say a prayer for those boots. They were special. What did Martensen say about them? Does he think they belong to the murderer?"

"I didn't tell him about them."

"Why not?"

"I wasn't supposed to be back there. He'd have pitched a fit if he knew."

"Do you think someone from the department saw them?"

"I think so. Gabe's got a good team. Even if Martensen is a horrible deputy chief, they'll find the killer." Pretending a bug flew past me, I waved my hand and removed the barrier. The crowd had almost doubled in size since I'd created it. "The committee members are hovering near the fireplace. I'm going to talk with them." Thoughts of Gabe rushed through my head. I closed my eyes and imagined them walking to my brain's door, ready to settle into the forefront of my mind, but I slammed the door shut before they entered.

"That's a good idea. They don't need to think this has anything to do with the festival."

"Nobody needs to think that," I said. I tapped Cooper's nose. "You stay here. I don't want you getting squished in this crowd."

He looked up at me. "Uh, that's not how this works. It's my job to keep you safe, not the other way around."

He'd stayed home the night before, but I couldn't remind him of that. Mr. Charming flapped his wings.

Stella jerked back. "It freaks me out every time he does that."

"It's his way of stretching," I said.

"I guess." She scanned the room again. "Look at all these people. Gossipmongers waiting for a bite of juicy gossip to chew on and spit out."

"Gossipmongers. Gossipmongers," Mr. Charming said. "Spit out. Spit out."

She raised her eyebrows. "He's so good at that."

"I wouldn't use those words." I eyed my bag on the floor and placed it on the table. "Don't let the gossipmongers get my bag."

She giggled. "No problem."

* * *

Deanna Cassidy connected with the magical world, but she wasn't magical, at least not by birth. She'd studied magic for many years and had become a practitioner of sorts. Somehow, the magical world opened for her, but she'd never told our secret. Humans like Stella considered her habits strange, and her clothing, akin to the Hocus Pocus movie wardrobe, over the top, but they believed her harmless.

I wasn't so sure.

"Abby, dear." She wrapped me into a hug. "How are

you?"

"I'm fine." I smiled at the rest of the committee. "I wanted to make sure you're all okay."

Damien Longwood, a shapeshifter with a soft heart for shelter dogs, spoke first. "I think we're all just shocked. Cornelius was hard to handle sometimes, but we're all sorry about what happened."

"We are. I am," Constance said. "I can't stop crying." Tears streamed down her face. Isaac slipped his arm around her shoulders and handed her a tissue. "It's just awful."

Damien moved to Constance's other side and patted her shoulder. He bumped his hip into hers, and she moved closer to Isaac.

I glimpsed Benedict Carrington check his watch. "It's half-past eight. I've got to be at work in fifteen minutes." He hugged Deanna. "If you hear anything please let me know."

"Will do," Damien said. "I need to get a move on as well. I've got a meeting in the office." He brushed his hand over Constance's shoulder. "If you need anything, call me."

"Will do," she said without even looking at him.

The rest of us chatted for a bit until Deputy Chief Martensen arrived with an update.

He waved his hands in the air. "All right. All right. People, please settle. If you'll all zip those lips of yours, I can make a statement."

The room silenced.

He sauntered over to the fireplace and shot me a glare. An officer followed behind him and placed a bench on the ground. Martensen stepped onto it. I covered my smile. The stout deputy chief was rounder than he was tall, and even with the stool, most of the room couldn't see him.

"Now, as you all know already," he said. He adjusted his

suit jacket. "Last night we discovered the body of Mr. Cornelius Stone."

They discovered the body?

The room gasped as if it was the first they'd heard about it.

"Did you catch the killer?" Someone from the crowd asked.

"We are working the investigation," Martensen said.

"Do you think it's a serial killer?" A woman asked.

Another woman gasped. "Oh, my! A serial killer?"

The crowd buzzed with chatter.

"Hold up, people," Martensen said. "We have no reason to believe a serial killer killed Mr. Martensen. Now, I can't tell you what we know, but I will say this. We are working hard to close this case. I don't want my town walking on eggshells thinking someone else is going to get killed. In the meantime, just go about your business, but as always, keep watch around you. I'm not saying something is going to happen, but prepare yourself, just in case." He nodded. "Now, I've got to get back to work." He stepped off the stool, and the crowd moved in for the kill before he escaped.

"Deputy Chief Martensen, do you have any suspects?" One asked.

He waved his hand in the air and pushed through the crowd, slithering out the door without another word.

Most of the crowd, including the rest of the committee, followed him out. Stella tapped my shoulder. "He said nothing of any substance."

"Not a thing."

"He just wanted to be the center of attention," she said. "Gabe would have been nose to the ground on this if he was here."

Gabe.

4

"Why are we here?" Cooper asked. "It's a crime scene. We're not supposed to be here."

We stood at the edge of the church, our eyes fixated on the body outline taped where Cornelius had died.

"Abs," he said.

"Yeah?"

"Are we just going to gawk at this or do something?"

I wasn't sure whether the scene had been cleared, so I'd stopped at the store and purchased two shower caps and a pair of rubber gloves. I slipped the shower caps over my feet and stuffed my hands into the rubber gloves. "I just want to look around."

Cooper sighed. "This is my nap time. I might not be at my best since I'm sleep deprived."

"You literally just woke up. Again. You'd have to stay awake for months to reach sleep deprived status."

"Cats require more sleep than other animals."

"Put on your big boy panties, and you'll be fine."

He grimaced. "Cats don't wear panties." His little body shook. "And I'm grossed out at the thought of it."

"Come on," I said, ignoring his babble. I checked behind us to make sure no one was around. "I'll put a barrier up so no one knows we're here, just in case."

"Good idea. They don't serve tuna in the slammer."

"Good grief." I twirled my finger and a glossy bubble surrounded us. I walked to the tape outlining where Cornelius died. "I was right here." I leaned up against the dumpster.

Cooper dry heaved. "Is that you?"

"Seriously?" I whipped around and stared down at him. "We're standing next to a dumpster. A garbage dumpster. It's not me. Geez."

"You ate leftover pizza for lunch. Pizza always gives you gas. I just figured—"

"I know what you figured," I said. "You don't have to explain." He was right though, it smelled like rotting eggs. "I smelled this last night too. I think someone threw eggs into the dumpster."

Cooper backed up and flung himself into the air. He landed on the rim of the dumpster. His little paws grasped the steel with such force his nails whitened. He stretched his head down and smelled. "Nope. Not the dumpster." He climbed off, using the side of the dumpster as stairs. "It's this way." Nose to the ground, Cooper searched for the smell. He scurried behind the dumpster. I followed behind him, watching as he stopped where I'd found the shoe prints. He flipped around. "It stops here."

"This is where I found sneaker shoe prints. Just one set and they went nowhere." I examined the ground, but the prints were gone. "Hold on." I rushed over to where Stella's prints had been, and the holes from her boot heels and the indention from the balls of her feet had faded but were still visible. "That's weird," I said.

"I think the scent is connected to the shoe prints," Cooper said. "Let me follow it the other way." He dropped his head again and sniffed his way to the corner of the church where I'd heard something fall to the ground and saw the mysterious figure. He sniffed back and forth around the edge of the church, exploring to the front and up the entrance steps. When he finished, he met me in back. "It stops here."

"How could a scent just stop?" I asked. "It's not like someone drove a car here, parked beside the church, murdered Cornelius, then took off into the mud. The car would have been here."

"There are no car tracks," he said. "And I don't smell exhaust. Whoever did this walked through the mud first."

"That makes sense. The person came from somewhere that way." I pointed to the muddied area. "Killed Cornelius, then ran past the side of the church when I arrived."

"And you transported yourself. Humans can't see magic, so you know what that means."

"Right. Whoever killed Cornelius is a magical."

He shook his head. "I can't believe I had to spell that out for you."

"You didn't. I can't follow a smell like you, and I already thought it was a magical because there's only one set of prints. That means the person appeared there magically."

"A lot of magicals can transport themselves. It's a mid-level witch trick."

I nodded. "What do you think the smell is?"

"Nasty. Foul." He dry heaved again. "Just thinking about it makes me sick."

"Oh, the drama. You just followed the smell and didn't even flinch."

"Because I was concentrating. Now that I'm relaxed, the nastiness of the smell is back."

"Whatever. Let's go. I don't want to mess up the scene any more than we might have already." Something on the ground caught my eye I walked toward the front of the church. I bent down and picked it up and brushed the dirt off the top. "Oh, no."

* * *

I poured myself a Diet Coke with lots of ice and opened my computer on my coffee table. Cooper snoozed on the top of the couch, his whiskers vibrating from his little snores.

I'd redecorated my apartment two months before Cornelius's death. I'd needed to keep busy to keep my mind off Gabe. I'd painted the walls a soft blue a tad lighter than a pair of faded jeans. I'd purchased a new rug for the living area and loved how the blues and creams matched my walls and couch. The remodel eased my nerves, but the effect stopped when I searched the magical web for the item I'd found at the church.

I read the information out loud. "The Fallon family crest is the Fallon family's way of announcing their superiority over other magicals. They wear their crest as amulets draped over their necks to show that superiority. They believe their superiority elicits power over other magicals. Their beliefs cause conflict in most magical cities, however, in the early 70s, residents of Holiday Hills refused to bow to the Fallon Family. Instead, the town worked together to banish them. Holiday Hills is the only town to act, and the family swore to destroy the town when least expected."

I studied the crest. It was dirty, but not to the degree that it had been left on the ground fifty years and just uncovered.

It seemed as if someone had just dropped it and kicked dirt onto it without realizing. "This can't be good."

Cooper jolted awake. "Did someone say tuna?" He shook his body and laughed. "I'm kidding, though I am hungry."

"Look." I shoved the amulet toward his face. "It's the Fallon family crest."

"And?"

"And I need to talk to Bessie." I stuffed the amulet into my back pocket as Cooper stretched. "Come on." I picked him up and held him under my arm.

"I don't tip," he said.

"What?" I walked into the hallway.

"If you're carrying me, you're my chauffeur. I'm not tipping you."

"That's fine."

I lived in an apartment above the Enchanted. Bessie owned the building and had cut my rent to almost zero when I needed a place to live after my divorce. My heart raced at just the thought of my ex-husband Zach. We weren't on horrible terms, but there were times just the thought of him made my blood boil.

Bessie had cleaned up all signs of the crowd. I set Cooper on the ground. Mr. Charming flew toward us. I extended my arm for him to perch. "Hello, Mr. Charming. How's our sweet boy?"

"Sweet Boy. Mr. Charming is a sweet boy. Kisses." He leaned to my mouth and tapped it with his beak. "What doing?"

"I'm here to see you and Bessie, of course."

Cooper hopped up on the counter. "I think she's in the kitchen."

"Mr. Charming loves Bessie. Bessie. Kisses." He flapped his wings and flew to the kitchen door, landing on the ground in front of it. He tapped his beak on it and said, "Hello? What doing?"

I opened the door for him. I'd planned to research shapeshifters transporting but hadn't had the chance, so I talked with Bessie about it before showing her the amulet.

"Oh, gosh." She wiped a coffee cup dry and set it on the metal shelf above the sink. "Every witch can transport, eventually, Abby. Most shapeshifters can as well."

"Most shapeshifters can transport?" I asked. "I thought that took years for them to learn." I glanced at Cooper gulping down a can of tuna. If he'd heard, which I doubted, he didn't care.

"Most of them don't have a problem with it. Two years before your mother passed, a wolf appeared in town. He shifted to his human form and attracted the magicals around him. Once he had a crowd gathered, he told them all he wanted to show them a parlor trick."

"And he what, disappeared?"

"He sure did. And he reappeared behind them. He offered every shapeshifter the chance to learn, for a price of course."

"And they paid it."

"Every single one of them back then. Of course, we've seen our shifter population grow in leaps and bounds since then. Many witches worry about them, but for the most part, the shifters here are kind souls.

"Someone with a kind soul didn't murder Cornelius."

"You're right." She tucked the towel into the top of her pants waistband. "Would you like a tea?"

"No but thank you. Bessie, I found something at the murder scene."

"Something that could lead to the killer?"

"Maybe. I'm not sure, but it could be a problem of its own or just nothing." I touched the amulet in my pocket.

She furrowed her brow. "What did you find?" She studied my face. "Are you okay?"

I removed the amulet from my pocket and held it up for her.

"You found this at the murder scene?" She took it from me and wrapped it in several paper towels.

I explained to her how I'd come across it.

The bell on the entrance door rang signaling someone had entered the store. "Let me get that." She turned around at the door and said, "Don't worry about the amulet, Abby. I'm sure it's a leftover from when they came here fifty years ago. And besides, the Fallon family knows not to mess with the witches of Holiday Hills."

I sure hoped so.

5

Stella splayed out on my couch and kicked off her shoes. "So, you're going to stay out of it, huh?"

I set the pizza box on the coffee table.

Cooper moaned. "Pizza again? You'll be up all night with heartburn."

Not all night, just the second half.

"I am." I opened the box and set a piece on a plate for Stella and one on a plate for me. I handed her the plate and shoved her feet off my side of the couch. "Martensen and I don't get along, and I don't want to deal with him."

Cooper sniffed the air. "Did you get anchovies? I love anchovies."

I ignored him.

She sat up and bit into the point of her pizza slice. She chewed while she talked. Stella's impeccable manners only surfaced when necessary, and I didn't care about manners when we were together either. "I know, but I think that's a load of garbage."

"Oh! That reminds me. Coop and I went and had a look at the crime scene and—"

She interrupted me. "Wait. I thought you were staying out of it?"

"I was. I mean, I am. I just wanted to look at those shoe prints again."

"Why?"

I shrugged. "I don't know. Anyway, there was this weird smell there. Like rotting eggs."

She'd just opened her mouth for another bite of pizza when I'd said that. "Gross." She set the plate on the table. "I think I'll hold off until you're finished."

"Sorry. It was just strange, but I followed it to the side of the church where I saw the shadowy figure."

"The shadowy figure lurked at the church's side, scraping its razor-like fingernails across the crumbling bricks, taunting Abby." She chuckled. "Sometimes I think I'd make a better writer than an editor."

"I wouldn't suggest it. Dealing with editors is a challenge. My point is the smell disappeared. One minute it's there, and the next it's not."

"Maybe it was something lingering from the restaurant down the street. That happens a lot."

"I don't think so."

"Are you saying you think the smell is associated with Cornelius's murderer?"

"I'm not sure."

"Abby, people all over town dump their garbage in the church's dumpster. Those things always stink. I'm sure you just got a whiff of something in there and as you put distance between you and the dumpster, it detached from your nostril hairs." She picked up her plate and set it on her legs. As she scooped her pizza slice off it, she said, "You should write some romance. All these cozy mysteries have you thinking you're some amateur sleuth." She chewed another bite and said, "Sorry honey, Hallmark isn't hiring."

I tossed my napkin at her. She laughed.

Cooper climbed over to me and sniffed my pizza. "I'm sure it's anchovies I smell." He scrutinized my slice. "But I don't see them."

"Do you like the sauce?" I asked Stella. "I got the one with ground anchovies in it this time."

Stella's eyes widened. She spit the food in her mouth into her napkin and placed the plate back on the table. "Is that what I'm tasting?" She shook her head. "I'm out. Got any chips?"

* * *

The dirty man with the clown nose appeared again in my dream. In the latest edition, I'd sat at my regular table in the Enchanted as I read through my latest manuscript. The front entrance bell dinged. I glanced up, and the clown nosed man walked in wearing a Chicago Cubs baseball hat. The rest of his outfit was the same. He sauntered over to me. I closed my laptop and jabbed my finger his direction. "Don't say it."

"Gabe's not coming home."

My blood raced through my veins. I flung my hand up and threw an invisible ball at his head. The ball exploded into a mass of deep red flames, creating a cloud of dust so thick it burned my eyes. I squeezed them shut. "This is just a dream. This is just a dream." When I opened my eyes, the man was still standing there, without a scratch or burn, as if I hadn't just tried to set him on fire.

"Gabe's not coming home."

I awoke to Cooper swatting my face with his paw. "Abby. It's a dream. Wake up."

I gasped when I saw his little eyes staring into mine. "Get

—" I'd almost hurled my cat off my chest and across the room, but I caught myself beforehand. "It was that clown nosed guy again." I shivered. "I don't like him."

"It's the pizza. The sauce's acid plays tricks on the body."

I shuffled to the kitchen for a glass of water. "It's not the pizza. It's my inner turmoil about Gabe and how he's not checked in at all for a while." I guzzled down the water. "Do you think something's wrong with him?"

"No. I don't think something's wrong with him. I think he's busy saving the world and doesn't have time to check in with his girlfriend." he hopped onto my kitchen counter and patted his cat food cabinet with his paw. "Since you're up."

"Fine. I don't think I can go back to sleep anyway so I might as well work on my book. I opened a can of tuna, scooped it into his bowl, and set it on the counter. I prepared myself a quick cup of coffee, then fired up my laptop. Three hours later I'd polished my last manuscript to its best version yet. I typed an email to my agent and sent it off to her.

I've struggled for success since going on my own as a self-published author over a ghost writer with a large publisher. The former publisher offered me a contract before, which I took, but things didn't work out, and we parted ways. They'd since asked me to write a different series, one without a magical element, but I hadn't decided. My agent thought she could sell my current series, including the book I'd had with the publisher, to another one, so I'd written three more to add to the series. I set my computer onto my coffee table and rubbed my eyes. A yawn escaped both Cooper and me. "Looks like we could use a cat nap," he said.

"I agree." I reached for the pillow on the opposite end of the couch, stretched out, and snuggled on my side with my arms wrapped around it. Cooper climbed onto my shoulder and snoozed there.

* * *

My cell phone woke me from a sound sleep. Cooper fell from my arm without waking as I stretched to the table to grab it. "Hello?"

"Ms. Odell?"

"Uh, speaking."

"Good morning. This is Mayor Howe. I'm sorry to call so early, but we must discuss the festival. Are you available this morning?"

About the festival? That wasn't good. I checked the clock on my cell. Six o'clock. Who calls someone at six o'clock if it wasn't an emergency? "Sure. What time works for you?"

"Can you meet me in my office in say, thirty minutes?"

"I'll be there. Mayor Howe, may I ask what about the festival you'd like to discuss?"

"We'll talk when you arrive. See you soon."

I tossed the phone onto the table and rubbed the back of my neck. "Great. Just great. I bet he's going to cancel the festival."

Cooper stretched his left leg out in front of him "Who?"

"Oz Howe."

He sat up and scrutinized my face with his dark, little eyes. "What did he say?"

"That he wants to talk to me about the festival."

"He didn't say anything about canceling it?"

"No, but he's going to. I know it."

He climbed off the couch. "We don't know what he wants, so let's just go and find out."

"I'll get dressed."

"Um." He flicked his small head toward the kitchen. "Aren't you forgetting something?"

I folded my arms across my chest and tapped my foot. "Seriously? You just ate a few hours ago."

"I have a high metabolism."

My fists clenched. I'd go broke spending money on tuna. "Fine." I stomped into the kitchen and opened the can, then dumped it onto a plate and shoved it toward him. "Eat fast. I don't want to be late."

"I always eat fast."

Twenty minutes later I sat in front of the mayor's desk with Cooper on top of my black boots.

Mayor Howe walked in from a door behind his desk. "Ms. Odell. Thank you for coming. I realize it's early, and I appreciate you getting here so quickly." He swung his hand behind him and closed the door with a flick of his wrist. Howe called himself a warlock. Most of the warlocks in town used that phrase over witch. Men could be witches, and supernatural books referred to them as so, but in Holiday Hills, they believed the term feminine, and stuck with warlock. "I understand you discovered poor Cornelius Stone's body."

"Yes, sir."

"I've been told you found a Fallon family amulet at the scene."

My voice shook. "I'm sorry?" I had told no one but Bessie about the amulet, and I knew she wouldn't share the secret.

"The Fallon family amulet. I understand you found it outside the church. Do you have it with you?"

Way to put me on the spot. "May I ask who told you that?"

"I'm not at liberty to say."

I straightened in my chair. "With all due respect, I haven't shared that information with anyone except a close friend as I didn't want to create any cause for alarm. I know that friend didn't share it with you or anyone else, so I would appreciate knowing where you heard this."

He leaned back in his chair. "Very well. Constance Ambrosia contacted me late last night. She's very concerned something's going to happen at the festival."

How did Constance know about the amulet? Had she been there without me knowing it? Was she the one who murdered Cornelius? "I'm not sure what Constance said, but I've discussed this with Bessie, and we both believe someone left the amulet years ago. The earth shifts, and it's come out of the dirt because of that." Weak, but it was the best I could come up with on the fly.

"Ms. Odell, as you are aware, this town has a history with the Fallon family. A very concerning history, and the town took their threat to heart. If they are coming back, we need to be prepared. With that and the fact that we have a murderer on the loose, having a festival isn't appropriate. We want to keep our citizens safe, especially the humans like your friend Stella."

My jaw stiffened. "Mr. Mayor, with all due respect." Cooper wrapped his front leg around mine. I glanced down at him. He shook his head, but I didn't care. "The fear of the Fallon family is the very reason we should keep the festival as planned. If we allow the fear to overwhelm us, we'll just make it worse. We shouldn't cancel the festival. We've put so much work into it already."

"I haven't decided yet, but I think I should address it. Do you have the amulet? May I see it?"

"I don't have it with me."

He nodded. "Are you sure it's from the family?"

"I don't know, but I assure you, I'll find out."

He rubbed his chin. "Very well. I'll give you a few days to do that. In the meantime, I'd appreciate this staying quiet."

Ditto. "May I ask how Constance found out?"

"I'm not sure. All she said was she didn't want anyone to know it came from her, so please keep that between us."

"Not a problem." I shook Cooper off the top of my shoe. "Thank you." We rushed out the door and back to the sidewalk in front of the city hall.

"Constance told him? How did she find out?" Cooper asked.

"I don't know, but you can bet I'm going to find out."

6

Bessie dropped her cloth on the stainless-steel kitchen counter. "Constance told him? How did she know?"

I shrugged. "I don't know, and he doesn't want me to talk to her about it."

"That's odd." She picked up the towel again and shook it, then folded it in half and hung it over the bar attached to the counter. "I hope Mayor Howe doesn't cancel the festival. Everyone's worked so hard on it."

"I know. If I can verify the amulet is a fake, we'll be fine." Maybe.

"How do you expect to do that?"

"I'm not sure, but I'll figure something out."

Cooper burst through the door panting as he raced toward us. He jumped onto the counter and caught his breath to speak. "There's a—"

A woman screamed. "He promised me!"

My eyes shifted to Bessie's. Glass smashed to the ground in the café. "Promised!"

Mr. Charming knocked the door open with his beak and

shook as he crash-landed onto the counter. "It's bad. It's bad. Mr. Charming. It's bad."

Smash! Bang! Smash!

"I've got it," I said and stormed out of the kitchen. Three people, all magicals, stood with their mouths hanging open watching Deanna Cassidy slam Bessie's glass flower vase to the ground, crushing it into tiny pieces. I yelled, "Deanna, enough," and I balled my fist, raised my arm, and flung it toward her, opening my fist as it centered on her. A blast of red sparks flew toward her.

She turned just as the sparks spun around her. The redness in her cheeks darkened to a greenish hue.

Cooper stood below me. His teeny mouth hanging open. He sauntered over to Deanna, sniffed her, tapped her with his paw, then flipped back to me and said, "Yup. She's the real deal." He sat on his hind legs and examined his paw. "Am I going to get warts for touching her?"

"Ribbit," Deanna said. She blinked. "Oh, hello, Abby. Ribbit."

"Oh boy. That wasn't my intention."

Cooper skirted over as the other two customers chuckled between themselves and froze with his three legs up as he stared at Deanna. He angled his head to the side. "Wow. How did you do that?"

I chewed on a fingernail. "I have no idea." A flush of heat zipped up my neck. "I haven't frogged a single person since my first witchy days."

Cooper eyed Deanna. "Well, you should fix her."

"Oh, right!" I flicked my hand and imagined Deanna as herself just in case my power messed up again.

Deanna morphed back into herself. She flipped her hands over several times, scrutinizing them with slitted eyes.

I patted my chest. "Woo. This is awkward."

Cooper side-eyed me. "How do you think she feels about it?"

Deanna's face darkened to a blood red and a scowl formed on her lips as she marched toward me.

Cooper raised his backside and hissed. "I'll be in the kitchen. Fake witches freak me out."

"So much for protecting me."

He meowed and scurried away. Mr. Charming flew to my shoulder. I assumed to offer his protective services. "Thank you, sweetie."

"What doing?" he asked.

I didn't have the opportunity to answer.

Deanna jutted her left hip to the side and clasped her hands on her hips. She tilted her head to the side and shook her head. "You did not just turn me into a frog!"

I cringed. "Yes, I did, but that wasn't my intention. I'm sorry. I meant to just stop you from destroying Bessie's. I didn't think you'd want the police here."

"It's okay. Just don't do it again. My skin turned wet and slimy." She shivered. Her gaze flicked upward. "As if I haven't had enough of Deputy Chief Martensen already."

Bessie peeked out from the kitchen, frowned at the mess Deanna had created, and twirled her finger. The mess disappeared as I led Deanna to a table. "You spoke to Martensen?"

She nodded. "He came by my place late yesterday. Wanted to know where I was the night of Cornelius's murder." She snorted. "As if I would murder someone without magic."

"Well, in his defense, Martensen's a human. He wouldn't know it was magic. So, are you a suspect?"

"I don't think so. I told him I went straight home after the committee met. Besides, what reason would I have to murder Cornelius? Sure, he was condescending and rude, and had an ego the size of Texas, but I got what I needed from him, and that's all that mattered. Though now I'm not sure what I'll do."

"What was it you wanted?"

"My pin the broom on the witch game. After the meeting, he assured me it was a go." She crossed her arms over her chest. "Now he's dead, and I don't know what's going to happen." She leaned forward in her chair. "Do you know how hard I've worked on that game just to have Benedict toss it out the window?" She sighed. "It's so disheartening."

"What do you mean?"

"That's what's got me so upset. He's taken over as committee head, with no approval, mind you, and he notified me to let me know my game's not happening. My game. He has no right. Cornelius promised." A flush of red creeped up her neck and settled onto her face. She stared down at the table but wouldn't make eye contact with me. "It's just so upsetting."

Bessie came over with two cups of hot tea. "Here." She set a cup in front of Deanna and the other in front of me. "This will settle your temper."

Deana studied the cup. "What's in this?"

"It's just earl gray. Nothing else." She turned toward me and winked.

I hoped she'd dropped a little truth spell into Deanna's cup. "Thank you, Bessie."

"Sure thing, sweetie."

I turned my attention back to Deanna. "I'm sorry. I know how hard you've worked on that game." I knew because that was all she had talked about for the last month. "I'll talk to Benedict. He can't take charge without a nod from me, anyway." I sipped my tea. "But I'm not sure I understand.

You said you talked to Cornelius after the meeting, but you also said you went straight home."

"Well, I went straight home after talking to him. That's what I meant."

"Had everyone already left?"

She blinked. "The meeting?"

I nodded. Was she stalling?

"Oh, I'm not sure. I mean, I talked to Cornelius outside. I had to use the ladies' room when we finished the meeting, so I did that, then hurried outside to catch him before he left. He was talking with Constance, but when I arrived, she stuck her chin in the air like she always does and stomped off."

"Do you know what they were talking about?"

She shook her head. "I'm sure it was about their breakup though."

"But you didn't notice anyone else still at the church?"

"I wasn't paying attention. I had a goal in mind, and I achieved it." She swirled her tea inside her cup.

"And how long did you talk to Cornelius?"

"Five minutes maybe? I wasn't timing it." She glanced around the café then narrowed her eyes at me. "Why are you asking me these questions, Abby? Do you think I had something to do with Cornelius's murder?"

"Of course not." I hoped my nose hadn't grown. "You know I'm responsible for this event. If I don't have a handle on my team, things won't go well. And the last thing we need is one of us being a suspect. I'm just looking out for everyone."

She lowered her voice. "Then you should have a talk with Constance. She's the one carrying a torch for Cornelius. She was a wreck when he dumped her. She told me she'd rather see him dead than with another woman."

I raised an eyebrow. "I thought she broke things off between them?"

She leaned her head back and laughed. "That's what she wants people to think, but he dumped her. He said he couldn't commit to one witch when there were so many to choose from. I hate to say it, but she deserved it. She wasn't good to him. Enchantresses aren't capable of love. I think Cornelius figured that out and moved on."

Ouch. Poor Constance. I disagreed with Deanna. Enchantresses could find love. It was rare, but it happened. Their breakup must have hit her in the heart. Enchantresses wrapped all men into their web of desire. It took a lot of strength for Cornelius to walk away from that. "That's awful for her. When did this happen?"

"Last week after the meeting. She told me they talked behind the church. He wanted it to be private, which is surprising given his tendency to show off." She smirked. "Seems fitting she'd murder him where he ended things, doesn't it?"

"Did you tell this to Martensen?"

"I had to. If she committed the crime, she should suffer the consequences." She blew on her tea and sipped it. "Oh, this is yummy."

Cooper looped through my feet. "Dang. She's not throwing Constance under the bus. She's stomping on her and then throwing her under it."

I pressed my lips together.

"What?" Constance asked. "You don't agree?"

"I think the justice system should punish Cornelius's murder. I just can't imagine it being Constance."

"Yet you asked where I was when it happened."

"Of course, I don't think you did it either." Thank God I

wasn't Pinocchio, or my nose would have grown a mile long by then.

"Most of the town despised Cornelius. His murderer could be anyone."

"Is there anyone you think wouldn't have done it?"

She bit her lip, then sipped her tea. "Let me think." She touched her fingertip to her chin. "Other than Constance or Isaac, I can't say."

"Why Isaac?"

"There was some mix up at work, and Cornelius accused Isaac of altering his digital timecard. He was up for a promotion, but he lost it when Cornelius went to their boss."

"When did this happen?"

"A few months ago."

"Did Cornelius get the promotion?"

"I believe so."

I had no idea, but that gave Isaac motive, and he hadn't mentioned it. Why not?

"I'm not sure Isaac could do it t. Kill Cornelius," she said.

"What makes you say that?"

"He doesn't have it in him. He's too soft."

I exhaled. "You'd be surprised what soft people can do."

Her eyes widened. "Are you accusing him now? I didn't mean to say he's the murderer. I just meant he had reason."

"You're the one who brought him into this. I'm just saying we can't assume anything about anyone."

She shrugged. "Maybe you can't, but I can." Her phone alarm dinged. "Oh, I must go. I have a client coming. I'm giving her a love potion. You know us humans. We're always looking for the right love connection."

I didn't have the heart to tell her those potions weren't long term, nor did I ask about the amulet.

7

I spent the rest of the morning researching the amulet, but everything I found said the same thing. The Fallon family loathed Holiday Hills and vowed revenge for being banished. But it had been fifteen years, and nothing had happened. I nudged Cooper who slept on the tabletop next to my tablet. "Hey, what if it's fake?"

My voice jarred him awake. He hopped onto his hind legs and stuck out his front paws as if defending himself. "It's mine!"

I laughed. "Were you dreaming?"

His body shook. "Uh, yeah. I was, you know. Saving you."

"It's mine?" I furrowed my brow. "You were fighting for a can of tuna again, weren't you?"

He hung his head. "Salmon. It's my worst nightmare too. I never get to finish the fight, so I never know who gets the can."

"Wow. How tragic for you."

He glared at me. "Don't be sassy." He stretched his front legs. "Why did you wake me up?"

I angled my laptop so the both of us could read it. "What if it's fake?"

"The magical internet isn't fake, Ab."

"No, not the internet. The amulet. What if it's not real?"

"Why would someone put a fake amulet by the church?"

"Maybe they wanted to scare Holiday Hills or stop the festival?" I clasped my hands and tapped my knuckles against my chin. "Or maybe they wanted Cornelius's murder to signal the revenge of the Fallon family beginning."

"I'm going with no on those."

"But it's possible." An idea popped into my head. "Why didn't I think of this before?"

"Oh no. I know we're heading into trouble whenever you say something like that."

I cocked my head and shook it. "That's not true."

He snorted. "Right. And I was a king before I became a familiar."

I gasped. "Were you?"

He rolled his little eyes. "Sarcasm. That was sarcasm."

* * *

It took about an hour to drive from Holiday Hills to Dawsonville. It should have been less, but the curved, hilly road scared most drivers into going twenty miles under the speed limit.

Cooper snoozed on the passenger seat while I pounded my fist onto my steering wheel and lost patience with the woman in front of me. "It's the peddle on the right!"

She slammed on her brakes. I swerved to the right to avoid hitting her. My car wasn't too close to hers, but she'd come to a complete stop, and I'd just reacted. My mouth dropped open to see a momma cat and four kittens cross the road. They must have been feral, but I hated they lived like that. I couldn't let it continue. I tapped my nose and wished them all to happy homes who loved their cats like I loved Coop. As each one made it across, they disappeared. Including the momma. I wondered what the woman in front of me thought about that?

My soul brightened. I couldn't perform that kind of magic often. There were rules to messing with the universe. If we changed too much, we set off the butterfly effect and changed the trajectory of everything. No one knew what consequences would come from that kind of change, but all magicals did it a time or two, when our hearts took over for our heads.

I kept right at the roundabout, made two lefts, and then I pulled into the small parking lot at the strip mall behind the outlet mall. "Here we are." I poked Cooper in the side.

He opened one eye. "I'm up. You don't have to poke me."

"Your eyes were closed. How could I tell you were awake?"

"Was I snoring?"

"Good point." He didn't sleep without snoring. "This guy is supposed to be good. Let's see if he can help."

He huffed. "Fine."

Magical Charm's door chimed as we walked in. An old man smiled from behind the counter. He brushed his few strands of hair from one side of his head to the other. As he stood, he adjusted his brown sweater. "Good afternoon. Name's Albus Mage. How can I help you?"

Cooper dropped his head and meandered around the store sniffing everything at ground level.

I smiled at the man behind the counter and said, "Hi," as I headed toward him. "I found something, and I'm not sure it's real. Would you have a look?"

"Sure thing." He pulled his chair close again and sat. "What is it?" He eyed Coop exploring. "That your familiar?"

"Yes, sir."

"Does he eat mice?"

"Mice?" Cooper dry heaved. "That's nasty."

I shook my head. "His food of choice is tuna, and from a can."

The man smiled. "Good to know. My familiar is a mouse, and he's wandering around here somewhere."

Just then Cooper hissed and jumped two feet into the air. He stretched out his front paws to grab hold of a glass shelf full of crystals, but he missed. Instead, his paws scraped against it and the crystals crashed to the ground.

I gasped. "Oh no! Cooper!" I rushed over, but by the time I got there, the shelf was back up and the crystals all where they'd been before. Cooper landed on all fours. I flipped around and saw the mouse sitting on the man's shoulder.

"We get a lot of cat familiars in here," he said. "Now, what's it you'd like me to see?"

I removed the amulet from my purse. I'd cleaned it up before leaving for Dawsonville, and there wasn't a speckle of dirt on the thing. "I found this on the ground outside our community church. I'd like to know if it's real." I handed him the amulet.

He flipped it over. "Fallon family crest. You must live in Holiday Hills."

I nodded.

"When did you find it?"

"A few nights ago."

"The night someone murdered that warlock?"

"Yes, sir."

He nodded. "I can understand your concern. Let's have a look."

He flipped over a large magnifying lens attached to his counter, pulled it close, and turned on its light. "Hmm." He nodded. "Ah." He rotated the amulet in a circle, hemming and hawing the entire time.

I bounced on my toes. Cooper sauntered over. I crouched down and picked him up so he could watch as well. He hissed at the mouse on top of Mr. Mage's head. "Stop that. He's one of us."

"Still a mouse."

I shook my head.

Mr. Mage shut the light off and moved the magnifying lens to the side. "I'm happy to say it's a fake." He turned the amulet over. "See this line here in the middle? It's barely visible, so look closely."

I bent close and looked but saw nothing. "I don't."

"Here, let me help." He set the amulet on the counter and tapped it with his finger. It enlarged to donut size. He pointed to a thin line. "Right there."

"I see it now! What is it?"

"It's the seam. Whoever made this did so in two parts. The Fallon's use a mold for the entire amulet. They require an exact match to the family crest. This line might be hard to see, but they'd know it was there. This isn't from them."

"You're sure?"

He chuckled. "Miss, I'm never wrong. Now, the question for you to answer is, why would someone make an amulet belonging to a banned family all Holiday Hills is afraid of?"

"That's what I'm wondering, but I'm going to figure it out."

"You think it's connected to that murder?"

"I found Mr. Stone that night, but I didn't find the amulet until the next day."

"Did you tell anyone?"

"Just someone I trust, but somehow word got out, and

now the mayor wants to cancel our mum festival. I can't let that happen. My mother started it."

He blinked. "Addie?" A smiled swept over his face. "You're Addie's little girl?" He laughed. "Well, not so little anymore! Abigail, right?"

"You knew my mom?"

"Sure did." He crouched down and moved something under the counter. "Here it is." He popped back up and set an old photo album on the counter. "There's something in here you need to see." He flipped through the old album's pages, each with worn plastic sticking to faded photos. "Here it is." He flipped the album around and pointed to a photo. "Right here."

A photo of my mother and Mr. Mage. My mom. My eyes swelled with tears. Though it had been a while since she had passed, the grief still sat in the back of my heart waiting to pound its way to the front. A lump formed in my throat. I swallowed hard but it wouldn't budge. The best I could choke out before sobbing was, "Oh, wow." Cooper wrapped himself into a rope around my ankles and rubbed his face against my leg. I breathed in, held it, then released it in hopes it would bring calm.

"I'm sorry," Mr. Mage said. "I thought you'd like to see it." He moved to close the book, but I put my hand on the page and stopped him.

"No, I'm elated to see it! It just caught me by surprise. I haven't cried about my mom in a while. I'm sorry."

He tilted his head to the side. "Honey don't you ever apologize for loving your mama. She was a wonderful woman." He placed his hand on the photo album. "May I show you another?"

"Please."

He flipped over to pages and pointed to a photo. "This is

just after she'd decided to bind your powers. In fact, she came here for some items she needed to do that." He smiled at me. "I'm assuming you know all about that?"

"Yes. She wanted me to live a human life. I don't think she knew they'd resurface after she passed."

"Oh, she knew. She said she'd be watching you and giggling when you couldn't figure out what was happening to you. She even set it up for your magic to come back through your nose. Figured it would show itself at her life celebration." He sighed. "Sorry, I couldn't make it. I just couldn't bear to see her that way."

"I understand." I brushed my fingers over the photo. I didn't remember the day, but that wasn't uncommon. We had a lot of days together. "May I take photos of these?"

He removed the photo. "How about you just take them? Addie would like that."

"Thank you."

He put them in an envelope and stuffed one of his cards in it as well. "You let me know if I can help with anything else, okay?"

"Will do. Thank you again."

Outside, Cooper said, "Who'd plant a fake amulet where Cornelius died?"

"That's what I'm wondering as well. But I'm calling the mayor to let him know it's a not real."

8

The mayor's phone went straight to voicemail. I left a message asking him to call me as soon as possible. Next up, speaking with Constance. I drove to her work, but according to her boss, she'd taken the week off, so I headed toward her house.

"Can't we eat?" Cooper asked. "I'm withering away here."

"Right. I can see your bones under all that fur."

"Contrary to popular opinion, I am not fat." He stood on his hind legs and patted his belly. "This here is all muscle."

"You're getting chonky."

"Chonky? Is that slang for chunky?"

"Yes."

"Rude.

I chuckled. "I won't be long, and then I'll get you two cans of tuna, okay?"

"Promise?" he asked.

"If you promise not to return it back to me."

"I can't make that promise."

"I figured. When we get there, I want you to stay in the car. If I need you, you'll know."

"I'm cool with that. I can take a nap." He stretched again. "I'm sleepy."

"Good grief."

Constance Ambrosia lived on the top level of a three-story walk up two streets off town square. She owned the building and had done a complete exterior remodel a few years before. The updated porch and double door steel and concrete front entrance stood out from the older bricked homes surrounding it. I rang her bell.

She spoke through the speaker. "Abby? Is that you?"

I stuck my face into the video doorbell. "It's me."

Steel and concrete aside, her heavy steps vibrated through the door. She rotated the lock and opened the door an inch. "Hi, Abby. I'm sorry. I'm not up for company right now."

Her swollen, red nose and eyes told me she'd been crying. I should have expected that. Someone murdered the man she loved. I moved to the side so she couldn't see my left hand, and whipped up a casserole dish of fresh, magically made shepherd's pie. I held it up to her. "I brought nutrition."

She opened the door. "Come on in." I followed her upstairs. She shuffled toward the back of the opened floor plan near the enormous glass garage door style window that led to an amazing deck, then fell onto her creamy white sectional. Steel, glass, and black beams highlighted the expansive space. Even her counters and cabinets were steel. The sleek, modern style looked fabulous, but not homey. I preferred homey over anything.

I set the casserole dish on the counter next to a container of gorgeous mums and sat next to her. She'd placed red, orange, and yellow mums in various spots around the large space. All as lovely as the one on the counter. "Is this yours? It's beautiful."

"I wish I could grow a mum like that. Isaac dropped it off for me earlier today. He thought it would cheer me up. The rest are mine. They're not as stunning as his, but they're coming along."

"I think they're beautiful. That was sweet of Isaac. So, how're you holding up?"

She yanked a tissue from the box beside her and wiped her nose. She glanced down at her gray sweats and teddy bear slippers. "I don't like anyone seeing me this way. Please don't say anything."

I zipped my fingers over my lips. "Not a word." I admired the long bead and chain eyeglass necklace. "That's lovely." I didn't intend to stay long, so I sat on the edge of the couch. "This must be hard for you."

She sniffled. "You have no idea. I don't even understand it." A tear trickled down her cheek. "I'm an enchantress. Men fawn over me everywhere I go. I'm not supposed to fall in love, and yet, I did. And with the most stubborn, selfish man in town!" She pulled her knees to her chest and wrapped her arms around them. "I just don't get it."

"Love doesn't give explanations. It just happens." I was a perfect example of that. I'd fallen for a warlock whose work ruled his life, and I trailed at a distant second.

"Well, love sucks."

I laughed. "You've got that right." I exhaled and loosened my stiff shoulders. "May I ask what happened between you two?"

"We broke up. What more I can say?"

I gave her a half smile. "He broke up with you because he wanted to see other women, didn't he?"

She looked up at me and blinked. "Who told you that?"

I shrugged. "It's a small town. The only people keeping secrets are the dead ones." I wished I could suck those words back into my mouth and start over.

She sighed. "Yes, it's true. A warlock dumped the only enchantress in town. When that gets out, it'll ruin me." She pulled another tissue from the box and dotted it into the corners of her eyes. "It had to be Deanna. She's the only one who knows. I told her in a moment of weakness after it happened. I shouldn't have. She's never been trustworthy. Especially with witches. Even so, I can't believe she betrayed me like that."

"I think she's just worried about you." I wasn't about to tell her how Deanna had pinned her as Cornelius's murderer. That was the last thing she needed to hear. My nose crinkled. I'd caught a whiff of something rancid. It wasn't my shepherd's pie, was it? It hadn't smelled bad when I whipped it up magically. I hoped I didn't mess it up. I'd always struggled with magical food recipes. "I think I might have cooked the shepherd's pie wrong. It doesn't smell right."

"Oh, that's not it. It's the mums. I think it's the flower food I use. Anyway, about Deanna." She folded the tissue and stared down at it in her hands. "It doesn't matter. After the last meeting, you know, the night he — someone murdered him, he tried to get back together. He apologized and everything." Her eyes traveled back to mine. "I said no. I was so angry with him. I wanted him to work for it, you know? Now I think if I'd said yes, maybe we would have left together, and he'd still be alive."

"You can't think like that. This isn't your fault."

"My brain knows that, but my heart doesn't understand."

"Did you two talk inside the church?"

She shook her head. "We'd stepped outside after the meeting to talk. At his request."

"Out front?"

She blew her nose. "Why are you asking all these questions, Abby?"

I folded my hands on my lap. "Because the mayor is worried about some things, and he's considering canceling the festival. I can't let that happen."

"Yes, it was out front."

"What happened at the meeting? Did anyone argue or have any issues?"

She shook her head. "No. Strange too, since that usually happened. But the meeting was quick, and I think Cornelius wanted it like that. We're so close to the festival start date, we only went over assignments. It lasted all of twenty minutes."

Was an appointment with his murderer the reason Cornelius cut the meeting short? Was he meeting them outside the church? Could that have been his killer? "Did Cornelius agree to Deanna's pin the tail on the witch game?"

She raised an eyebrow. "Not at the meeting. He said he'd discuss it with her later. I think that was just a way of delaying her throwing a fit. She rushed out and got on him about it right after we'd finished talking, too. I didn't want to listen to it again, so I left."

"Did he say why he'd cut the meeting short?"

"Not a word."

"Who was still there when he asked you to talk outside?"

She gazed off toward the front door. "I'm not sure, but I don't recall anyone walking out while we talked. Other than Deanna, of course." She exhaled. "Do you think someone from the committee murdered him?"

"I don't have any thoughts on it. I'm just trying to understand the events of the night."

"Well, after we talked, I ran into an old friend, and we spent time together." She smirked. "If you know what I mean."

A rebound man? It wasn't impossible to believe considering her enchantress ways. I didn't want nor need to address that, so I redirected the conversation. She'd told the mayor about the amulet. That meant she'd either put it on the side of the church or gave it to someone who did. "You know about the Fallon family, right?"

She furrowed her brow. "I think I've heard of them. Aren't they the family banned from here?"

"Yes. Did you know any of them?"

"That was before my time. I moved to Holiday Hills the year after that all happened. Why are you asking?"

Why was she lying? I kept going to see what she'd say. "You'll hear about this, anyway. I went back to the scene the night after the murder. I found an amulet on the side of the church. I did some research, and it's the Fallon family crest, but the amulet is a fake."

She tilted her head to the side. "Where did you find it again?"

"On the side of the church. I saw whoever killed Cornelius turn that corner around the church when they saw me. It's possible he or she dropped it, but I can't figure out why anyone would have a fake Fallon amulet."

"Oh, I doubt the killer had it. What would be the reason?"

"That's what I'm trying to figure out."

"Did you tell the police?" she asked.

"No, but the mayor found out somehow. I went to Dawsonville before coming here. Mr. Mage at the Magical

Charm examined it and verified it's not real. I left the mayor a message, so I'm hoping he won't cancel the festival, but I just don't know."

Her doorbell rang. She clicked an app on her phone. "Yes? Hello?" She studied the screen. "Is anyone there?" She laughed. "Hold on." She set down the phone and smiled. "Your kitty just rang my bell. I think she wants in."

Cooper would be livid to know she thought he was female. "You don't mind?"

"Not at all." She hit the buzzer and the downstairs door opened.

"I'll let him in," I said. Cooper strutted in like he owned the place.

I sat again, and he climbed onto my lap. "It's getting deep in here. Thought I'd come and check it out."

I patted his head. "Good boy."

Constance stood by her enormous kitchen bar. I could have fit five of my kitchens in it and it would still have room. "I appreciate the shepherd's pie, but I need to take a shower, and I don't know. Get on with my life, I guess."

I lifted Cooper and stood. "Just one more quick question."

She exhaled and released it with a big sigh. "Fine."

"Can you think of anyone who might want Cornelius dead?"

She laughed.

Cooper's little body stiffened in my arms.

"Just about everyone in town. No one liked him except for me."

"I understand that. I mean had he had any issues with anyone recently?"

She shrugged. "Just the festival committee that I know

of." She held up a finger. "Deanna was adamant about that game, and then there's what happened with Isaac."

I pursed my lips and acted surprised. "What happened with Isaac?"

"You haven't heard? Cornelius stopped him from getting a promotion at work. I can't believe you didn't hear."

"I haven't. Was Isaac upset?"

"He didn't mention it to me, but Cornelius said they'd argued about it." She shuffled to the door and opened it. "Thank you for the food, and for checking on me. If you learn the mayor's canceled the festival, please let us all know right away."

"Of course."

As she closed the door, Cooper said. "Time to find out why she's lying."

"How are we supposed to do that?" We got into my car and headed home.

"How else? Cast a spell."

"I can't cast a spell on her. I'm only allowed to do that when there's no other option. You know that."

"You did it to Deanna. What's the difference?" He climbed onto my dashboard.

"I didn't intentionally cast a spell over her. I only meant to stop her from ruining Bessie's things."

"Being your familiar is so boring."

"Consider yourself lucky."

9

I climbed into the attic above my apartment and sorted through a box of my mother's things. She had maps from all over the world. I had an atlas and a Holiday Hills map, but I wanted a world map too. Just in case.

I moved all the junk I'd piled onto my coffee table to the floor. Three books, a candle, the TV remote, hand cream, and a bag of chips. I spread out the Holiday Hills map first.

Cooper sat on the couch next to me. "I wish I could swing the crystal."

"You could try, but I'm not sure if it would work. First, you're too short, and second, you don't have thumbs."

"You have no idea how frustrating that is. You'd think I'd be a polydactyl cat. It's still not a thumb, but at least it's an extra finger."

Poor Coop. He might have had a wealth of skills to protect me, but sometimes he wanted the little things. "Here. I'll hold it. You grab it and swing it. That's the best I can do."

"No. I want to try."

I shrugged. "Okay." I handed him the string. "There you go."

He held the crystal in his mouth and dropped it over his tiny leg. I watched in amazement. What was his plan? He wrapped it over his leg several times until the crystal was short enough for him to stand beside the map and lean over to swing it. He never ceased to amaze me.

"This is outstanding," he said. He whipped his paw and swung the crystal with so much force it did an almost complete flip, stopping as it smacked his little nose. His eyes crossed, and he fell backward.

"Oh!" I jumped from the couch and caught him before he hit the floor. I lugged him back onto the table and checked his eyes.

"I'm fine," he said. His head lobbed to the side. "Is my nose bleeding?"

I examined the patient. "Doesn't look like it. Here, let me untangle you."

"Just my body, not my arm. I'm trying again."

"Are you sure?"

"I can't let a little crystal beat me. What kind of familiar would that make me?"

I smiled. "Got it."

I untangled him, and he went for it again, that time swinging it with less strength. The two of us focused on the fake amulet. The goal was to find out where it came from and who it belonged to.

It stopped and stuck to the map. Cooper smiled. "And I'm awesome."

I glanced at the map and then at him. "It stopped on our apartment. We already know the amulet is here. I'm not sure why it would stop here. I focused on finding where it came from."

"Oh, is that what you wanted me to do?"

I leaned into my couch. "What did you focus on?"

He jumped from the table to my side, holding up his little paw with the crystal on it. "I might have been distracted by tuna."

"Cooper Odell!"

He rubbed his face across my leg. "I'm a cat. My priorities are innate. I can't control them."

I unwrapped the crystal from his arm and held it over the map, swinging it forward and letting it take control. It swung to the right and landed across the street from my apartment at the bead store. "The bead store?"

"Don't ask me. What do I need beads for? I couldn't grab one if your life depended on it."

I reached across the table and grabbed my cell. "Let me check their website." I typed the name into the search engine, and it popped right up. I swiped through the site searching for anything related to jewelry making in-house. "Look. Annealing. It's how they melt silver to shape it into jewelry."

"Wild. That means someone made the amulet at the bead store."

"Right." I checked my watch. "Shoot. It's already seven o'clock. How did that happen?"

Cooper's eyes widened. "That means it's tuna time!" He raced to the kitchen. "You coming?"

I dragged myself to the kitchen. A wave of exhaustion swept through my body. I yawned. "Wow. I'm beat, and it's barely night." I opened the can of tuna, dropped it into a bowl, water included, and set the bowl on the floor. "There you go. Eat slow."

"Right. Like that'll ever happen."

I dragged myself back to my couch and fell onto it in a

heap of Abby exhaustion. I snatched the remote from the floor below me and powered on my box, clicking on Hallmark. It didn't matter what was on. I'd watch it.

* * *

The man with the clown nose showed up again. His dirt smell infiltrated my nostrils. His He hadn't changed clothes, but they appeared dirtier than before.

I shook my finger at him and glared. "Go away. I know what you're going to say, and I don't want to hear it, okay? So, just go."

He stepped closer. "Gabe's not coming home."

"I told you not to say it!" I drew my arm back and launched a ball of fire straight for that stupid clown nose. "Go away!"

The flames landed on the man and fizzled to nothing.

I dropped to my knees and cried. "It's only a dream! It's only a dream!"

"Abby, wake up!"

I awoke to Cooper breathing in my face.

"The clown nosed dude again?" he asked.

I nodded.

He licked my cheek. "That blows." He stepped to the side and snuggled between my shoulder and the couch. "But it's just a dream."

"Coop, what if it's not? What if it's a sign, and Gabe really isn't coming home?"

"Only one way to find out." He climbed onto the back of the couch. "Make contact."

"But what if—"

"You can't what if this. Just do it and deal with what happens," he said.

"I've tried. He's not come."

"Maybe he was busy? He is on a special assignment. It's been a few weeks since your last attempt. Try again."

"You're right. I just don't want to be disappointed."

He meowed. "That must be why you're always so cranky."

"I am not always cranky."

"Whatever you say. Now, are you going to do it or not?"

I exhaled and said, "Fine," at the same time. I sat with my legs crossed on the couch and focused on Gabe. His convincing smile. His muscled arms. His broad shoulders. I shook my head to focus on something other than his physical appearance. "Gabe. It's me. I need you. Please, come to me."

I opened my eyes, begging him to be there, but he wasn't. I leaned back into the couch and groaned. "It didn't work. Maybe the clown nosed guy isn't a just a manifestation of my insecurities about Gabe? Maybe he's real?"

"If he's real, why not just come to you and say, *hey, dude's done. Move on?*"

I furrowed my brow. "That's a little harsh don't you think?"

"Not if it's the truth."

"We don't know if it is," I said. Though it sure felt that way.

"And that's my point. Stop worrying so much about Gabe and live your life. He said he didn't know how long he'd be gone. It could be years. You don't want to be that weird old witch with a cat. Stop being anti-social."

"I'm not anti-social. By the way, most witches have cats."

He meowed. "Good point, but you know what I'm saying."

My couch vibrated. I pressed my hands flat into it. It

vibrated again. I glanced at the table, and it shook as well. As soon as it all began, it stopped. "Did you feel that?"

He'd been completely still. "I thought it was you."

"Me what?"

"Nothing," he said.

"What's happening?"

"An earthquake maybe?"

"We haven't had an earthquake in a year," I said.

"Seems time then."

The vibrating returned with double the intensity. The map slid off my coffee table. My TV switched off. The lights blinked. The candles on the shelf across the room crashed to the ground.

Cooper hissed. "Take cover!" He dove off the couch back and raced under it, still yelling something inaudible.

The vibrating stopped again. I exhaled though I hadn't realized I'd held my breath. "Wow. That's so weird." I crawled off the couch and peeked under it.

Cooper stared at me. "You think it's done? For good?"

"I don't know, but I don't think we're in any danger. Come on out." I giggled. "You're supposed to be protecting me, and here I am, the brave one."

He scooted out and gazed up at me. "I like earthquakes about as much as you like mountain men wearing clown noses."

"I get that." The ground shook again. Cooper lost his balance and toppled over onto the floor. I gripped the table to steady myself. My knuckles turned white. "It's not done!"

He dove under the couch again. "Sweet baby Jesus! We're going down!"

The lights flickered on and off, then something loud snapped. Maybe a transformer outside? The table slid across the floor with me still attached. The couch lifted off the ground and slammed back down. I screamed. "Cooper! Cooper!" I let go of the table and crawled to the couch, the shaking knocking me over three times in the short distance. "I'm here!" I stuck my hand underneath, searching for him. He dug his front claws into my skin. I yanked him out just as the shaking ceased. My heart raced, and the intense pressure in my ears knocked me off balance. Nausea swirled in my stomach. I fell back onto the floor holding Cooper close to my chest, breathing hard and fast. "We're okay." I patted his entire body checking for injuries. "We're okay." I kept him there for a while, feeling his heart pounding just as hard as mine.

Minutes later, he opened his eyes and peeked around the apartment. He detached himself from me and hissed. "Uh, Ab? There's someone here to see you."

10

I squeezed my eyes shut. "I'm not looking."

He climbed off my chest. "I'm serious. You need to look."

I shook my head. "No. It's the mountain man, I can feel it in my bones."

"It is a mountain man, but it's not what you think. Open your eyes, Abby."

I opened one eye, but only a little. The second followed on its own. I gasped. "Gabe?"

The person looked a little like Gabe, but scruffier and dirty and with hair I'd only seen in my dreams. His eyes were his tell. I'd know them anywhere. I pushed myself up, trying to fix my messy hair and make myself presentable. Heat flashed through my entire body. My heart raced again, but for a different reason. "Is it really you?"

"It's really me, Abby, but I can't stay. I tried to come earlier. I'm sorry, it just wasn't possible."

"Where's your clown nose? Is it really you in my dreams?"

"Clown nose? Dreams?"

I nodded. "In my dreams you're wearing a clown nose." My excitement waned. I clenched my fists. "Why do you keep telling me you're not coming home?"

"That's not me, honey. I swear.

"I didn't think it was until now. Everything about you is the same. Even your clothes. You referred to yourself in the third person." I hadn't noticed the mountain man's eyes. Could he have been pretending to be Gabe? Was my dream a sign of danger?"

"Someone's impersonating me. That's why I'm here. Don't believe them. It's a trick. They're trying to hurt me by hurting you."

"I've missed you so much!" The shock of him looking so rough, so unlike I was used to, faded, and I rushed to him.

He stopped me before I made contact. "No, I can't. They can't know I've been here. I've stayed too long as it is." He exhaled and smiled. "I love you."

"I —"

He disappeared.

Cooper rubbed against my leg. "Did he really look like the guy in your dreams?"

I nodded.

"What's up with that?"

"I don't think I want to find out."

* * *

Sleep evaded me all that night, but once the frustration and confusion over what Gabe had said had settled, I worked on the festival. His words left me with no option other than to go on as if everything was fine, even though it wasn't. I didn't understand any of it, but I'd learned the Magical Bureau of Investigation cared nothing about feelings, especially mine. Fighting that would only frustrate me more, so I refocused. I left the mayor a second message asking him to contact me as soon as possible and sent text messages to the entire committee requesting a meeting the next morning at the Enchanted. Cooper had dozed off a few minutes after Gabe disappeared. Not wanting to wake him, and before I was able to focus, I cried to myself. Texting Stella about it was impossible. She'd think I'd lost my mind. But she did call me.

"Did you feel that?"

"You felt it too?"

"I'm sure all North Georgia felt it. It registered as a 2.4, the highest we've ever had."

"And I thought it was Gabe."

"What?" she asked.

I backpedaled. "I thought it was his love for me pounding out of his chest."

She laughed. "You're hilarious. Have you checked on Bessie?"

"I haven't. I should do that now."

"Good idea. I won't be at the Enchanted tomorrow. I'm meeting with an author. He's not happy with my suggested changes to his story. Says I'm defiling his art. I'll show him what a true defiling is."

I laughed. "Probably not a good idea for business."

"I know, but a girl can dream, right? Talk to you later."

I nudged Cooper awake. "It wasn't Gabe."

He peeked at me through only one eye. "What?"

"The earthquake. It wasn't Gabe."

"Then I guess you don't have to worry about what the guy said."

"What guy?" I asked.

"The guy who showed up here looking like Gabe without showering or shaving for a year. If it wasn't him, it's no big deal." He closed his eye and snored a second later.

But it was Gabe? Wasn't it? Who else could it have been? And why such perfect timing? Unless, of course, the earthquake was a cover. But who would do that? Who would pretend they're Gabe? Who would infect my dreams with anxiety and fear? And why?

* * *

The next morning Isaac rang my bell. Our meeting wasn't for another thirty minutes. I'd just finished showering. "Give me a sec," I hollered. I threw on my clothes for the day, a pair of black leggings, a long, burned orange cardigan with a green silk blouse underneath, and a pair of black boots, and answered the door.

"Hey," he said. "I'm sorry to just stop by uninvited like this, but I won't make the meeting this morning, and I wanted to make sure we talked."

I opened the door for him to come inside. "Oh, is everything okay?"

He set his work bag on the floor. "It's good, yes. It's just that Cornelius's murder has caused some issues at work. I've had to take over a position I wasn't prepared to handle, but the good news is it's a promotion."

"I'm sure you have mixed emotions about that."

"Yes, I do. The police came by my place last night to question me, but I was still at work, so I'm going to run by there and see if I can help."

"They wanted to question you?"

"I'm sure they're going to question everyone on the committee. I live closet to the church. Hey, I ran into the mayor yesterday. He said he's thinking about canceling the festival. Is this true?"

"It is, but I won't let it happen."

"What's going on?"

"There's a rumor about the—"

He interrupted me. "It's not the amulet, is it? He's not thinking about canceling because of that."

I nodded. How had word of the amulet gotten out? Had Constance told him? "He's worried we're in danger."

"The library needs this money. They'd close without our donation. He knows that. He's the reason the city stopped funding the library in the first place," he said.

"I know, and I promise, I will not let him cancel this. How did you hear about the amulet?"

Cooper moseyed over and leaned against my leg.

Isaac glanced down at him. "I stopped by Constance's place yesterday to check on her. She mentioned it. I'll be honest, I left her and went looking for the mayor. I didn't exactly bump into him."

"Was this when you dropped off the mum for her?"

He nodded. "Did you see it?"

"I did. It's lovely."

"It's my fertilizer. I'm telling you, the stuff is a miracle worker. It's almost how I want it too. Just a few more tests, and I'll be done."

"That's great. What did Constance tell you about the amulet?"

"Just that she spoke with the mayor and that she was worried it had something to do with Cornelius's murder."

"Did she say what?"

He shook his head. "I think she's just being hyper-sensitive right now. She lost the love of her life, and that's rough on someone, but especially on an enchantress."

"You're probably right." I twisted my mother's black

diamond ring around my finger. "When did you leave the meeting the other night?"

"The committee meeting? I talked to Deanna a little about her event and then I left, so not too long after it ended."

"I'm sure it upset her to have her game approved by Cornelius and then nixed by Benedict."

"Cornelius never approved the game."

"Oh, she said he approved it that night after the meeting. I guess I just assumed everyone knew."

"How would we know? Someone murdered him before he told us. I doubt he approved it. He rushed us through the meeting because he said he had another appointment. It ended at around eight-forty, eight-forty-five. He didn't stick around when it finished."

If Cornelius had told no one he'd approved the game, how would Benedict know? Had Deanna made that up? It was possible. She was desperate for that game to be included, so lying about Cornelius agreeing after his murder could have been her way of getting it included. "He spoke to both Deanna and Constance outside. Did you hear their discussions?"

"No sorry. I know Constance chased after him, but none of them were outside when I left."

"And you're sure he didn't approve Deanna's game during the meeting?"

"Positive. She tried to discuss it, but he cut her off. I think it's a good idea, not having it in the festival. It's inappropriate considering the concept." He glanced at my couch. I hadn't cleaned up after the earthquake. Surely, he noticed.

He checked his watch. "Anyway, I've got to run. Don't want to clock in even a second late or they'll dock my pay.

They're watching our every move lately. Can you shoot me an update after the meeting?"

"No problem. Thanks for stopping by." I closed the door behind him and spoke to Cooper. "Interesting, huh?"

"You think Constance is involved with Cornelius's murder, don't you?"

11

"How could I not? She lied to me about the amulet. She told the mayor about it before I'd even said anything to anyone, and then she also told Isaac. Why would she do that knowing I'd find out?"

"Grief causes people to do strange things," he said.

"She's not people. She's a magical."

"Magicals are people too. Unless they're me. Then they're just a cat starving while he waits for breakfast."

"Is that a hint?"

"Yes."

I made his breakfast and added a scoop of salmon just because. "What if Constance had the amulet for whatever reason, and then it fell out of her purse when she ran after murdering Cornelius?"

"Could be true. Might not be."

"You're always helpful."

"My job is to keep you safe, not be helpful." He dove into his breakfast like it was the only meal he'd had all year.

"Should we talk about what happened during the earthquake?"

He lifted his head from his bowl. "I'm little and vulnerable. It could have crushed me into a cat pancake."

"Drama king."

He stuck his head into his bowl again and ignored me. When he finished eating, he rubbed his paw across his mouth then licked it.

Gross.

He licked his lips. "I think Deanna's up to something. She lied about her game. That's suspicious. Besides, she doesn't like cats. What's wrong with cats?"

I held back a laugh. "She's allergic to cats. I'd stay clear too."

"Allergic. Hateful. Same thing. Find out why she lied."

"She probably lied because she knows I'm in charge, and I can make the final call on whether her game's in or out."

"And what's your final call?"

"Out. Pinning brooms on witches sounds awful."

"Imagine if it was pin the tail on the cat. That would be awful."

* * *

Benedict Carrington stood at the counter chatting with Bessie. "Good morning, Abby." He glanced at the clock hanging over the kitchen door. "I think everyone else is running late."

Bessie poured me a cup of coffee, dropped a cube of sugar into it, and topped it off with cream. "Here you go honey. Any damage from the earthquake?"

"Nothing I can't fix. What about you?"

"All's good with me."

"We had an earthquake?" Benedict asked.

Bessie chuckled. "You must be a sound sleeper."

"I am when I'm in human form. Wolf form? Sleep isn't an option."

I pointed to the corner opposite the fireplace. "How about we sit over there? We can chat before the rest of the committee arrives."

He smiled at Bessie. "Have a great day."

I waved at Mr. Hastings as I walked by. Roger Jameson, another regular, shuffled in as we sat. I waved a hello to him as well. "So," I said as I sat with my back to the door. Benedict had taken the seat facing the entrance. "I'd like to talk about the night of Cornelius's murder."

"Okay." He pursed his lips and crossed his leg over the other. "I'm not sure what for, but sure."

"Did you stay after the meeting ended?"

"Is this about the mayor wanting to cancel the festival?"

"You heard about that too?"

"I think we all have. Word gets around quickly. I was at the gas station last night and heard people talking about it there."

I needed to get to the mayor's office as soon as possible. "We're not canceling the festival. Did you hear the reason?"

"The murder, of course. At least that's what I assume. Is there another reason?"

I nodded. "You haven't heard about the amulet?"

He furrowed his brow. "Amulet?"

I explained the situation.

"Why is everyone so paranoid about that stupid revenge promise? If the Fallons wanted revenge, they would have cursed the town and gotten it by now."

He had a point. "I agree. Tell me, did you stay after the meeting?"

"Yes. I had to lock up. I'm always the last one to leave.

You'd know that if you came to the meetings." He gave me a half smile.

Ouch. "Are you sure no one was there?"

He nodded. "Inside, yes. I'm sure. If you're asking about outside, I can't say. I don't walk the perimeter of the building. I just check the bathrooms and lock the doors. I always check the back entrance as well. But I don't do that outside. I can only lock from the inside. I don't have a key to the back door."

"Did you have another confrontation with Cornelius that night?"

He pulled back his chin. "What? No. No. Not at all. In fact, we talked after our argument here and worked out the issue." He removed a notepad and pencil from his bag and flipped through the note pad's pages, then rotated the pad my direction. "We agreed to split the duties once the festival began. I created this list and went to him with it. I had to keep my ego out of it, which trust me, wasn't easy. But we both agreed it would be easier for the volunteers and make it easier for us to split the duties and work together."

The bell on the entrance chimed.

"When was this?"

"I'm not sure. I guess around three that day? Maybe a little later?"

"And did you tell anyone?" I asked.

"We didn't get the chance. He told me he had to leave the meeting early. I didn't want to jump in without an explanation, so we planned on sending an email. It just didn't happen, obviously."

"What about after the meeting?" I asked.

"Like I said, he had to cut out early. Once Deanna stopped hammering him about her ridiculous game, he left."

"Deanna mentioned you told her you're the committee head now, and you canceled the game," I said.

He blanched. "She what?" He shook his head. "That's not at all what happened. I emailed her and told her Cornelius and I had worked things out, but given his murder, I asked if she would support me as committee head. She said she would if I approved her game. I have the emails. I can show you."

"Did you cancel her game in the festival?"

"I can't remove something from the plan if it's not already a part of it."

"Can you forward the emails to me?"

"Sure."

"Did you email anyone else?"

"I emailed Isaac. He never responded. I didn't tell Deanna I'd approve the game, and I really doubt Cornelius did."

"Where did you go after the meeting?"

He leaned forward. "Do you think I have something to do with his murder?"

"I'm just asking questions."

Someone coughed behind me. "I'm pretty sure that's my job."

I jerked my neck toward the familiar voice booming from behind. "Deputy Martensen. What a pleasure." It wasn't a pleasure.

Benedict snorted.

"Ms. Odell. A word."

I eyed Benedict. He raised his eyebrows and mouthed. "Don't turn him into anything."

I crisscrossed my finger over my chest. I followed Martensen outside, practicing my smile, though it hadn't mattered. I snarled anyway.

He eyed my face. "I see you're upset I asked to speak with you."

I pressed my lips together then made a popping sound with them as I opened them. "Deputy Martensen, I may ask questions of my committee regarding the murder of another committee member."

"Of course, you can, but we both know that's not what's going on here. Let's just cut to the chase, okay? Now." He spread his legs to hip width and crossed his arms over his chest. "I know the former chief allowed you to play detective, but that's not how I do things around here. I'm telling you to keep your nose out of my investigation."

"That doesn't seem all that kind."

He inhaled then blew it out straight into my face. His breath smelled like minty eggs. "I'm not in the mood for sassy sarcasm, Ms. Odell. Now, either you do as I say, or I'll throw your butt in the slammer. I don't much care who you're dating. Not that he's ever coming back."

My jaw dropped. Before I said anything, Cooper had climbed up Martensen's pants and dug his claws into the side of his leg. Martensen howled and kicked his leg out to the side. Cooper dropped out, hissed, then opened his mouth and drove his needle-sharp teeth right through Martensen's pants and into his meaty leg. He held on for dear life as the deputy chief shook his leg.

"Get this beast off my leg or I'll have him euthanized!"

A small crowd gathered on the sidewalk, all of them magicals. They pointed and giggled as Cooper hung there, swinging back and forth with each leg thrust.

"I said get him off me!"

"Coop, stop!" I yelled.

He released his murder grip and dropped to the ground. "Nobody puts Abby in the slammer." He brushed the back of his paw over his face, then spit out a string from Martensen's pants. "Nobody."

Martensen glanced down at his pants, grunted, then eyed Cooper. When he drew his leg back, I held out my hand and said, "No!" I flung my wrist in a circle, and Martensen dropped to his knees. The crowd went silent when one of them made a snapping sound.

"Ouch, that's got to hurt," Cooper said.

"My knee! Call 911! I think I broke my knee."

The crowd lost interest and went back to whatever they'd done before. I dialed 911 and waited until the ambulance showed. We didn't speak another word to each other. After the drama ended, I headed back inside, already exhausted and in need of a long nap.

Bessie rushed over with a cold cloth. "You're redder than a tomato, honey." She patted my head with it.

"I didn't do that," I said. "I wanted to turn him into a mouse, but I didn't even get the chance. Someone in the crowd must have done that."

She smiled. "Yes, someone in the crowd." She winked.

I gasped. "Bessie!"

"Honey, you're family. No one messes with my family."

enedict and I didn't get to finish our conversation, but I did get to address a few things about the festival with the rest of the committee. After I finished, I asked them to speak with me one on one. I began with Deanna.

"Are we going to talk about Benedict wanting to be committee head again? If so, I vote no."

"Benedict didn't drop your game from the festival, Deanna. As far as he knew, Cornelius didn't add it in. Benedict just didn't agree to put it back in. Tell me the truth. Did Cornelius tell you he'd allow the game?"

Her eyes darted around the room. "Yes."

Cooper did crazy eights between my legs.

"That's hard to believe. Everyone on the committee is worried that game will be offensive to witches, even the shifters. No one wants the game in the festival."

"Why is it offensive? It's a game. If witches are that easily offended, they don't have to play."

"That's not how this works. You've been on this committee for years now. As far as I can remember, you always had some game with a hint of jealousy toward magicals in it, and they've approved none of them. Maybe when you spoke to Cornelius again, and he said no, you got mad, and things escalated."

Her mouth fell open. "Are you accusing me of murder?"

"As far as I can tell, you were the last one to see Cornelius alive. At some point, Deputy Chief Martensen will come to that conclusion as well. Are you prepared?"

"I didn't kill him." Her eyes pooled with tears. "We had our talk. He approved it. I swear. It might have been just to appease me in the moment, but I don't care. I got my approval. Why would I murder him when what's happened is exactly what I would have expected? Wouldn't I have wanted everyone to know he approved it? Don't you think I would have found joy in his having to tell the committee?"

"What time did you leave the meeting?"

"I'm not sure. I wasn't paying attention."

"Do you know why the mayor wants to cancel the festival?"

"The Fallon family amulet. I know. I also know half the town is prepared to fight him on it. He won't cancel the festival. No one is afraid of the Fallon family and their ridiculous amulet." She checked her watch. "Now, as always, I must run. I have a client appointment. But Abby, you're looking at the wrong female committee member." She flicked her eyes toward Constance and then marched out.

I spoke with Constance next. "Why did you lie to me about the amulet?"

Her face reddened. "I didn't lie to you."

"Yes, you did. You told the mayor I found it at the church, but there was no way you could know that unless you watched me pick it up. And how did you know it was the Fallon family amulet in the first place? It could have been a token for a video game machine at the pizza place. I could be wrong, but it seems the only person who would have known about the amulet would be the person who murdered Cornelius." That wasn't entirely true, but I wanted to see how she would react.

Cooper had pranced into the kitchen but raced back over.

She stepped back and placed her hand over her heart. "I did not murder Cornelius! How dare you accuse me of that!"

Cooper draped himself over my feet.

"I'm not accusing you of murdering anyone. If you were there when I found the amulet, you'd know where I found it."

"I wasn't there when you found it. I swear."

"Then how did you know about it? And why did you tell Mayor Howe?"

She exhaled. "I cast a direction spell to lead me to Cornelius's murderer."

"And it led you to me?"

She shook her head. "No. It led me to the amulet."

"When did you cast this spell?"

"Right when I found out it happened."

"And why did you tell the mayor about it?"

"Because I thought if word got out, I'd know who killed the man I loved. I thought the killer would react to knowing someone found the amulet."

"That doesn't explain how you knew I had the amulet."

She adjusted the collar on her brown and gold striped blouse. "I was keeping my eye on it with that spell. The spell alerted me to movement. When I looked, you had it."

"Why didn't you report the amulet to the police?"

She raised her eyebrow. "And say what? I'd cast a spell and found something connected to the murderer?

Martensen would have committed me to a night on the psych ward."

I couldn't argue with that.

"Abby, why would I kill the man I love?"

"You've lied to me twice, Constance. About the amulet, and about the breakup. How can I trust you?"

"I admitted to lying about the breakup, and I didn't lie to just you about it. I lied to everyone. It's important to maintain my reputation."

Lying to the entire town didn't get her off the hook. I worked the same technique on her I'd tried on Deanna. "Look at this from my view. Cornelius breaks up with you, the only enchantress in town. You have a reputation to maintain, remember? And then a week later, you're seen following him outside after the meeting, and not even an hour later, he's dead. What would you think?"

Tears filled her eyes. "It wasn't me."

"Then who was it? Who were you with that night? Can they verify it for you?"

"Who I was with is nobody's business." She glanced at the ground and then back up at me. "Don't you wonder why the amulet showed up at a murder scene?" she asked. "An amulet for a family intent on destroying us? Maybe Cornelius was their first victim, and the amulet is their calling card?"

"I thought that as well until I discovered the amulet is a knockoff." I eyed the tiger's eye beaded necklace hanging down her sweater. "They made it at the bead store. You wear a lot of beaded necklaces."

She exhaled and tugged on my arm. "Come this way." She dragged me to the restroom at the back of the café.

Cooper followed behind. He squeezed through the door and frame right before she closed it.

"What's going on?" I asked.

"Fine. I made the amulet, all right? Please don't tell anyone. I didn't mean to upset the mayor."

"Why on earth would you make an amulet from a family that hates this town?"

She leaned against the sink. "Because I was desperate and confused. I didn't mean for it to end up on the ground like it did. It was just to scare Cornelius. He once told me he feared that family more than anything. I figured if he thought they were back, he'd want my support. He'd need me."

"So, you dropped it on the side of the church? I don't understand."

"No. I dropped it in his pocket outside after the meeting. It must have fallen out of his pocket after I left."

I jutted out my left hip. "Why would you do that if he'd asked to get back together?"

She yanked a paper towel from the canister and dabbed her eyes. "He didn't, okay? He told me he was leaving to meet someone else. He was in love with someone else." She dropped her face into the towel and sobbed.

Cooper rubbed my leg with the side of his head. "Maybe you're right? Maybe it's her?"

Constance only heard meows. I wasn't sure what to do, but I couldn't just leave her like that, and I couldn't tell her I believed her, because I wasn't sure what to believe. Admitting that gave her even more motive to kill Cornelius. Would she have done that if she was his killer? I just didn't know.

I told her I'd give her a few minutes and left her in the bathroom crying. Cooper and I aimed for Damien. I'd barely spoken with him since Cornelius's murder.

He closed his laptop. "Hey Abby, I bet I'm your next interview about the murder, eh?"

"Interview?"

Cooper laughed. "You're some private eye."

"Everyone knows you like to investigate crimes in town. I'm assuming it's because of your relationship with Gabe."

"Yes, well, I wouldn't say that."

"So, what's going on?"

"Can you tell me about the night of Cornelius's murder?"

"What do you want to know?"

"Anything and everything you know." I exhaled.

Bessie set a cup of tea in front of me and gave Damien a purple and green liquid I couldn't identify. "Thank you," I said.

"Sure thing, honey. It'll give you the energy you need. You look exhausted."

"That's because I am exhausted."

She retreated to back behind the counter.

"Okay, yeah, so that night? The meeting was short. I'd arrived along with Cornelius. He told me the meeting would be quick because he was meeting someone."

"Did he say who?"

"No, but he adjusted his jacket lapels and strutted into the church, so my guess is it was a lady."

"Go on."

"He updated us on what was going on, said he had to run, shut Deanna down about her game and that was it."

"Did you stick around?"

"Nope. I'd gone to the bathroom right before Deanna started on about the game again. By the time I got back to the room, they were gone, so I left."

"Was anyone outside?"

He nodded. "Cornelius and Deanna were arguing. I wouldn't get involved in that, so I darted to the side and snuck away." He rubbed his five o'clock shadow. He'd kept that look for as long as I'd known him. "I wouldn't tell anyone about this, but I heard Deanna say she'd kill him if he didn't approve her game."

My heart skipped a beat. "She threatened him?"

He stumbled over his words. "I mean, I guess. But it's Deanna. Only humans take her seriously. Those magic tricks she does? They're nothing like witches. Cornelius would have killed her first. No question."

"Where did you go after the meeting?" I asked.

"I'm working the night shift at the shelter. I had to be there by nine, so I went straight there." He raised his eyebrows. "I can verify that. I already did with the police."

I shook my head. "It's fine." I drummed my fingers on the table. "Who do you think murdered him?"

He shrugged. "You know how Cornelius was, how he treated people. It could have been anyone.

13

"**M**r. Mayor, this is Abby Odell. I've called you several times but haven't heard back. The amulet is a fake. There's no reason to cancel the festival. I can verify this, but I need you to call me back. Thank you." I pounded the end button on my phone. "Jerk."

"Jerk. Jerk." Mr. Charming stood on my table munching on blueberries Bessie put out for him.

"Don't say that," I said. I pointed to his blueberries. "Say blueberries. Yum."

"Blueberries. Yum." He flapped his wings and hopped to me. He leaned his beak toward my face. "Kisses? Mwaah!"

"Mwaah!" I replied.

Bessie placed a chicken salad sandwich next to my laptop and a small bowl of tuna on the other side for Cooper. She patted Mr. Charming's head. "You're so sweet, giving all those kisses."

"Kisses?" he asked. "Mwaah!"

She chuckled. "It took forever to teach him that, yet he can repeat embarrassing and inappropriate things after hearing them once."

"It's his gift." My cell phone dinged. "Just a sec," I said and read the message from the shelter. "Damien punched in on the shelter's computer at nine PM. He could have stuck around and murdered Cornelius, but it would have to have been quick."

"That would have to be very quick." She sat across from me. "How's the manuscript coming along?"

I closed my laptop. "They're done. Well, they were done, and I sent them off, but now I'm going over them again and making changes. I have a call with my agent in," I glanced at my watch. "Five minutes. She's going to be angry. I've made none of the changes she wanted."

"She'll get over it. They're your books to change. Not hers."

"Maybe."

Mr. Charming hopped to me again. "What doing?"

"What doing? I'm whining. That's what doing."

"Whining. Whining." He flew off the table and in circles around the café. "Whining. Kisses? Mwaah."

"That bird's got issues," Cooper said. He jumped off the table and headed back into the kitchen.

My cell rang. "It's her," I said and answered the call. "Hey! I'm — really? That's great! I've made a few changes again. No, I'm not done yet, but I will be soon. I promise." I smiled at Bessie and gave Cooper a thumbs up. "Okay. Is that normal? Wow. Yes, I will. Thanks." I ended the call.

"That was fast."

"She knows an editor at one of the big publishers. She won't tell me which one, but she said she showed him the drafts, and they want them. Even the first self-published one. And she thinks she can get me a fifty-thousand-dollar advance."

Bessie's eyes widened. "That's amazing!"

"It kind of is, isn't it?"

A Holiday Hills police officer opened the café door. He held it opened while Deputy Chief Martensen hobbled in with crutches stuffed under his armpits. A large brace covered the leg he'd fallen on.

I swallowed and the pressure in my throat landed in my stomach, did a flip, and settled.

He hobbled over to me. "Ms. Odell."

"How's your leg?" I asked.

"It's my knee, and it's sprained, but that's it."

"I'm sorry about what happened."

He exhaled. "You're going to need to get that cat under control."

With perfect timing, Coop sauntered out of the kitchen and toward us. He meowed.

Martensen glared at him. "You keep that thing away from me. You understand?"

Cooper jumped onto my lap and snuggled in. "I'm showing him how loving I am to people who don't mess with my witch."

I smiled. "I think he was just protecting me," I said to Martensen.

"You don't need protection from the police."

"Is there something I can do for you? I can prepare dinner, or make you lunches? Run some errands? I feel awful." I didn't want to do any of those, but I had to offer, or I'd feel guilty forever.

He shook his head. "The wife will take care of me. I'm just here to let you know you can stop sticking your nose into my investigation. We just made an arrest. The community is safe once again."

"You made an arrest? Who?"

"I'll be making that announcement soon enough." He

hopped to the right and headed for the door. "You have a nice day, Ms. Odell."

"You, too." I whispered a spell to read his mind. "Powers that be, reveal to me what I need to see."

"That was weak," Cooper said.

"Shh. I'm trying to listen."

Martensen's mind revealed, *that evil little cat is going down.*

"Oh," I said.

"What?" Cooper asked.

"Shh."

I don't know what Gabe saw in that woman. He probably left town because of her. She begged for me to tell her I've arrested Constance. Like she needs to know anything.

"Oh! He arrested Constance!"

Bessie popped up from underneath the counter. "Constance? Really?"

"Guess he thought like you," Cooper said.

"Not really." Especially not about you.

I gathered my things and stuffed them into my backpack. "I'm going to the jail."

"There's no way they've finished with her," Bessie said. "She only left here two hours ago. Give it some time."

"You're right, but I need to know what's going on."

She pulled out a chair and sat beside me. "Do you really think Constance murdered Cornelius?"

"He dumped her. She loved him. She's an enchantress. She thinks it'll ruin her if word gets out about how they really broke up."

"Benedict and Cornelius had words in my café that very day."

"Benedict said they'd worked it out," I said.

"Did he prove it?"

"No, and I asked him where he went after the meeting, but he never answered."

"So, he could have lied about them working things out and killed Cornelius thinking he'd get the position," she said.

"And he said he'd emailed a few of the other members about it, so maybe?"

"Anyone else?" she asked. "I'm torn. I can't imagine one of the committee members committing murder, but who else could have done it?"

"The entire town. But as for the committee, I don't think Damien did it. He's the gentlest shapeshifter I've met, and he was at the shelter. They just confirmed it. Everyone's claiming to either not know when they left or has just given an estimated time the meeting ended, but I know it ended before five past nine because that's when I got there."

"And you saw something, yes?"

I nodded. "I'm certain now. I saw the killer run around the corner of the building. I must have just missed seeing the murder happen."

"And they dropped the amulet there to distract the police," she said.

I shook my head. "Constance made the amulet across the street. She wanted to scare Cornelius into getting back together. It must have fallen out of his pocket as he walked behind the church."

"Oh no. That makes things worse for her."

"If she's the murderer, it's supposed to be worse for her."

"Of course," she said. "I don't understand something. Why would Cornelius be going that way after all that rain?"

"It was the quickest way home, but everyone said he had to leave to meet someone or for an appointment. So maybe the appointment was that way as well?"

"Or maybe they were meeting at his house?" she asked.

"Right. I heard something interesting about Isaac. Did you hear about him not getting a promotion because of Cornelius? Something about digital timecards?"

She pursed her lips. "I recall something, but that was months ago."

"Word is Cornelius discovered Isaac altering his card and reported him. Cornelius got the promotion and Isaac didn't," I said. "Isaac told me he got promoted. What if he murdered Cornelius for that promotion?"

"Oh, honey. I just don't know. Like I said, I'm torn. Everyone on the committee has worked together for years. They may not always get along, but I can't imagine one of them would resort to murder."

I could. Magicals and humans no longer surprised me. "I need to find out what happened to Constance. Why they arrested her."

"You can't transport yourself there. They've got cameras," Cooper said. "They'll see you."

I groaned. "What if I make myself invisible?"

Bessie smiled. "I'm not sure that's a good idea."

"Not to offend you, but you suck at that. Last time you tried, the pizza guy saw you with that face mask plastered all over your face." He laughed. "When he dropped the pizza on the floor and ran screaming! Good times."

I furrowed my brow. "Rude."

"I speak only truth."

"It's all about focus," Bessie said. "If you can't concentrate on what you desire, it won't happen, or it will happen wrong. That's how magic works. That's why they say never perform magic when you're emotional."

When I was emotional was about the only time I wanted to perform magic. "How can I find out then?"

"I'm sure a magical from the department would tell you," Bessie said. "Why not just call?"

"I could do that."

Cooper swiped his hand over his ear. "Get out!"

I stared at him. "Uh, everything okay?"

"I've got an ear worm and it's driving me crazy."

Bessie chuckled. "Those are the worst."

I leaned back in my seat. "You've got worms!"

He shook his head. "No, Abby. I have an ear worm. A song stuck in my head. Not the whole song, just a few of the lyrics."

"What song?"

"There's a hole in the bucket dear Liza, dear Liza." He shook his head and swatted his ear again. "Hours. I've been singing it for hours."

"Isn't that a nursery rhyme?" I asked. "And why is that called an ear worm?"

"Yes, it's a nursery rhyme written in the early seven hundreds. Harry Belafonte released it as a song in the seventies, maybe? I can't remember. I can sing one part, and that's what I've got stuck in my brain."

"Who's Harry Belafonte?" I asked.

"I can't even," he said.

"Oh, I love Harry Belafonte," Bessie said. She hummed the words to the nursery rhyme.

He dropped from a sitting position and rolled onto his back then fell onto the floor and landed on all fours.

"I can't help that I don't know who the guy is." I grabbed my phone and googled Harry Belafonte. "He's ninety-five years old! You don't know him personally, do you?"

Bessie pointed to herself. "Me? No. I've never met him. Maybe I should introduce myself?"

"I was talking to Cooper."

"Oh. Well, that's possible."

Cooper licked his paw. "Maybe. I've been around a long time."

"That's crazy. I've always thought you were from the 80s. You used to have that valley girl talk down pat."

"I'm male. All testosterone, baby."

"On that note," I said. "Let's go home. I'll call the department and see what I can find out. The human way might just work."

"Keep me posted," Bessie said. "I know you'll figure it all out."

I hoped so.

* * *

I spoke with the jail guard who assured me Constance was in her cell. He even held out his phone so I could hear her crying. I felt awful, and I just wanted to find the killer more.

I threw on my pajamas and plopped onto the couch. "I don't want to do anything." Cooper didn't respond. I doubted he heard me over his snoring. I flipped through TV channels without paying much attention. Mostly, I thought about Constance and Cornelius. My cell phone rang. I checked the caller ID and groaned when I saw it was Deanna. She probably wanted to discuss her game. Again. I clicked answer. "Hi, Deanna."

"Abby, I need to see you. It's important."

"Deanna, if this is about the game, I—"

"It's not about the game, I promise. Listen, I don't want to do this over the phone. Can you meet me in a half hour?"

"Is everything okay?"

"Meet me at the church in thirty minutes, okay?"

"Deanna, what's going on?"

"I know who killed Cornelius," she whispered.

"What? Who?"

"It's someone from the committee, but that's all I'll say over the phone. I don't want them to know you know. You could be in danger like me."

"In danger? I don't understand."

"Please, just come. I need protection, Abby I'm scared. The killer knows I know."

"Okay, I need you to listen to me, and do what I say, all right?"

"I have to leave my apartment. It's not safe here."

"I'll meet you at the church. Do you have magic to unlock the door?"

"I can try."

"I'll put a protection spell over you. Do one yourself as well. Do you understand?"

"I'll try. It might be too late. I have to go."

"I'll be—"

She hung up.

I eyed Cooper. My obnoxious old fashion ringtone always shocked him awake. "We need to go. Deanna said she knows who murdered Cornelius, and she thinks she's in danger."

He yawned. "She's making that up. It's about her game. She's so focused on that thing nothing else matters."

"I don't think so, Cooper. She's very upset. I can hear it in her voice." I stood. I need to put a protection spell on her. I closed my eyes and focused on my breathing, then repeated the spell three times. "Elements of the sun, elements of the night. Protect Deanna with your light. So mote it be." I nudged Cooper. "Come on! We need to go." I rotated in a circle and stopped when my clothes had changed into a pair of jeans and a black sweater.

He stretched. "I knew you'd say that. A familiar's work is never done."

"Yes, your life is hard."

"That's the truth. Do we have to rush? Your protection spell will keep her safe."

"I hope so. You ready?" I bent down and scooped him into my arms.

"Let's do this."

I transported us, but we didn't end up at the church. "Darn it. Why can't I ever get it right on the first try?"

"You have to work on your transportation power." He examined the aisle. "And the dog food aisle. Is that a hint?"

"Not at all, and it's transporting." I squeezed my eyes shut. "Let me focus."

"Yes, focus," he said. "You aimed for the church and we're at the grocery store." He meowed. "In Alpharetta, Georgia."

My right eye popped over. "How do you know it's Alpharetta?"

He flicked his little head toward the front of the aisle. "See that banner over the windows? Alpharetta Publix. Best Store in Georgia."

"Oh." Heat rolled up my neck. I curled my shoulders forward hoping to shrink myself invisible. "Candy Corn's been in the back of my mind all day. I guess it took over at just the right moment."

"Focus, remember?"

"Right. Okay." What was wrong with me? Why couldn't I get my head right?

I tried, but that time we appeared at Cooper's vet. I smiled down at him. "What?"

Cooper stiffened like a brick. "Sweet baby Jesus. The one

place I hate more than anything." His body shuddered and stiffened again. "Get me out of here, quick!" He hissed and screeched. Hate didn't touch Cooper's feelings about the vet.

I squeezed my eyes shut. "The church. The church. Take us to the church!"

"In Holiday Hills," he said. "Not another awful vet!" He shivered in my arms.

"Oh, right. The church in Holiday Hills."

Boom! I opened my eyes. "We're here." I raised my hands to the starry sky. "I did it!"

"Uh, Abby? I think we're a little late." He pointed to the church steps.

"Oh, no."

"It's going to be a long night," he said.

Deanna Cassidy lay splayed backwards on the church steps with a garden fork stuck in her chest.

14

Patrol officer Remmington Sterling arrived. He shook his head with a slight laugh as he approached, but when he saw Deanna on the stairs, the laugh faded. "Abby." More head shaking. "What is it with you finding dead people all over town?"

"I don't mean to, but this one is my fault."

His eyes widened. "You did this? You killed Deanna?"

"No! That's not what I meant."

"She's the magical ghost whisperer." Cooper coughed up a hairball. "Oh, sorry. That one hit me just right."

"Coop, stop," I said.

"My bad."

"Then what do you mean it's your fault?" Officer Sterling asked.

"Deanna said she was in danger, but I didn't get here in time. It's my fault she's dead."

"Did you put a protection spell on her?"

I nodded.

"Then it's not your fault. It was just her time. You can't control that, Abby."

Couldn't I? Had I transported us correctly, we could have made it. We could have stopped the murderer. "It feels like I should be able to."

"You can't." He turned toward Deanna. "This isn't good. Martensen is going to lose it. You know he's looking for any way to arrest you."

"That's why I called you and not 911. I thought you could handle the situation." Officer Sterling was a warlock with a unique ability to alter perceptions through imagery. It was his strongest power. As a warlock, it had its advantages.

He exhaled. "Tell me what happened first."

"She called me and asked me to meet her here. She said she knew who the killer was."

"But she didn't say who?"

I shook my head. "She was afraid. She thought the killer was coming for her."

"The killer knew she knew?"

I focused on Deanna's face. I sighed. "She thought so." I set Cooper on the ground. "I should have tried a stronger spell, but she said she'd put one on herself as well. I thought she would be okay."

"When did you talk with her?"

"About thirty minutes ago. I tried to get here sooner but there were technical difficulties."

He raised an eyebrow.

I sighed. "I transported us to the wrong place first."

"Twice," Cooper said.

"Hush," I said.

Officer Sterling laughed. "Is he giving you a hard time?"

"Always." I glared down at my cat. "And it's not the right time."

"I'm just trying to lighten the mood," Cooper said.

"It's not working."

He rubbed his head against my leg. "I'm sorry."

Officer Sterling studied the surrounding area. "And you're sure it was her you talked to?"

"Yes."

"Okay," he said as he nodded. "Gives me a clear time of death. Did you see anyone else when you arrived?"

I cringed. "No. I shut my eyes when I transport. It makes me dizzy."

"I saw something," Cooper said.

I glanced down at him. "Hold on. Cooper saw something."

"A shadowy figure sprinted on all fours around toward the back of the church. It had a tail."

"He saw a shadowy figure sprint on all fours around toward the back of the church. It had a tail." I set my eyes on my familiar. "Why didn't you tell me that before?"

"When exactly did I have the chance? We got here. You called Sterling, and he showed up. That was, what? All of two minutes? Besides, I'm here to protect you, remember? If I had told you, you would have chased after it."

"A wolf?" Sterling asked.

Cooper shook his head. "Worse. I'm not sure, but I think it had horns."

"Horns?" I asked.

"Did he say a wolf with horns?" Sterling asked.

"Yes," Cooper and I said in unison.

"Sounds like a rabid werewolf."

"Or a shifter with a disguise," I said. "Officer Sterling, Deanna said the killer is someone from the festival committee."

"Great," he said. "That gives us a narrowed suspect list."

It wasn't great. It wasn't great at all.

* * *

"Decaf or regular," Bessie asked. I'd called her and asked if we could come by her place. I needed to get my head straight and work through what I knew. The mayor had returned none of my calls, and with Deanna's murder, the odds of the festival happening bordered on slim. If even.

"Regular is fine. I don't think I'll get any sleep."

Mr. Charming unlatched his cage and crawled out. He climbed to the ground with his claws and beak and hobbled to me. Cooper climbed onto the back of Bessie's couch.

"What doing? Mr. Charming loves Abby. Kisses?" He hopped onto the couch and reached his beak toward me. "Kisses."

I gave him a smooch on his beak. "Abby loves Mr. Charming." His sweet demeanor eased the rock sitting in my stomach, but not by much.

He tilted his head to the side, leaning almost completely over. "What doing? Coopie doopie doo! Coopie doopie doo!"

Cooper grunted. "Why couldn't you have named me Bill?"

"Billy willy, what a nilly?" I asked. "I'm sure others could think of something better."

He narrowed his eyes. "You've made your point."

Bessie returned. "Now, tell me everything." She handed me a cup of hot coffee.

It warmed my hands and smelled like heaven in a cup. Just smelling the brewed scent would have been satisfying, but I needed a full throttle caffeine blast to make it through the night. I gave her the details and ended with, "She said Cornelius's murderer is a committee member."

"Well, first, let's focus on the positive. Remmington is such a nice young man, protecting you like that. When Gabe returns, he'll be grateful. Now, let's discuss what happened to poor Deanna. Maybe we can figure out who she's talking about."

That's what I needed for many reasons, but also because I didn't want to think about Gabe. I'd done my best to distract myself from the clown nosed mountain man who looked a lot like him, Gabe's warning, and my insecurities about our relationship. "I think she might be right. Cooper and I both saw something with four legs leaving each scene. And I thought I saw the horns the night of Cornelius's murder. It could be any of the committee members. They can all transform into someone or something else."

"That's true, but it's also possible she was mistaken. Maybe she thought it was another person, but the killer thought she knew it was them?"

"She seemed adamant. Besides, we don't have many werewolves in Holiday Hills, and as far as I know, the ones we do are healthy. If it was even a werewolf."

She sat in the chair opposite the couch. Mr. Charming hopped from the couch and flew the short distance to the back of her chair. He climbed onto her shoulder and rubbed the side of his face into her hair. "Mr. Charming loves berries."

Bessie held out her hand and a bowl of blueberries appeared. She set it on the coffee table. "Here you go sweet boy." She shrugged when she saw me staring at her. "At my age that whole personal gain thing goes out the window. What matters is convenience." She adjusted her position in her seat. "And you put a protection spell on her?"

Tears streamed down my cheeks. "It didn't work."

"Honey, it's not your fault. If we could alter fate, your mother would be sitting here with us."

"I know." I sipped the coffee again. The warm liquid slid down my throat, offering me a touch of comfort with its familiarity. "We could do a return spell. Have her come back and tell us who murdered her."

"Oh, no," Bessie said. "It's too early for a return spell. She's being processed right now. That could take weeks, even months. And who knows, if it's her destiny, she may have been placed into another body and already reborn. We can't disturb the afterlife this soon after her demise."

"What about Cornelius? Is it too early for him too?"

"I'm afraid so."

"I feel helpless."

"You're not. You have me, and Cooper, and Mr. Charming, and Goddess knows many of the magicals in town are here for you."

"Good berries," Mr. Charming said.

"I hate to be a bother, but can you whip me up a can of tuna?" Cooper asked. He climbed onto the coffee table and stared at me. "I don't want poor Mr. C. here eating alone."

I pulled Bessie's trick but with tuna. "Benedict is a shape shifter. His primary form is a wolf. Can a shifter get sick and morph into something worse? Something with horns?"

"Most shifters can shift into anything they desire, but Benedict? I don't see it."

"What if he's ill? He could shift into something with horns then right?"

She shook her head. "I don't see Benedict shifting into something evil."

"Why not?" I asked.

"If I remember correctly, his family took an oath to shift into only wolf and human form. They had some issues in South Georgia where they used to live. They took the oath and most of the family scattered around the world for a fresh start."

"That doesn't mean he isn't sick, or he didn't go back on his oath."

"You'll have to do the research, but I believe the oath came with magic from the powers that be." She gazed off toward her front window. "It might have been the Barrington family and not the Carrington family. I'm not sure. It was a long time ago." She sighed. "Oh goodness, my brain doesn't work like it used to. But remember, Damien Longwood is also a shifter, and I don't think he took an oath like that. And then there's Isaac and Constance."

"Constance was in jail."

"Witches can escape jail with the flick of a finger."

"Right. I called and she was still there, but that doesn't mean she didn't astral project herself to the church and murder Deanna. I'll ask Officer Sterling about that. But Damien? He has a solid alibi for the night of Cornelius's murder. He was at the shelter. They already confirmed that." I sipped my coffee. It had cooled, but not enough to need a warmup. "I need to speak with Benedict again. He said he and Cornelius had agreed to share duties for the festival, but there's no proof of that. And he was the last one at church that night. What if he asked Cornelius to stay, locked up, then murdered him? He could be the shadowy figure I saw."

"Do you really think he would murder Cornelius over a committee head position?"

"I think people have done worse for less."

"Maybe, but I think you're wrong in suspecting Benedict. Aside from his oath, like I keep saying, I just can't imagine any of the committee doing that after all these years."

I finished my coffee and stood. "I need to go back to the church. I have to see what's going on and talk to Officer Sterling about Constance. I'm sure a magical at the department cast a spell to keep her from escaping. That eliminates at least one committee member. Coop, let's go."

Cooper's head popped out of his bowl. "Oh, man. I knew you were going to say that." He gazed down at the miniscule bit of tuna left uneaten. "Until we meet again."

I leaned over and hugged Bessie then planted a smooch onto the top of Mr. Charming's head. He was too busy with his blueberries to care.

15

I transported us straight to the church. "Figures," I said. "I get it right this time."

Deputy Chief Martensen stood just a few feet away, his back to us. He leaned on his crutches.

"We'd better get out of here. Transport us somewhere else," Cooper said. "If he sees you, you're toast, and who knows what he'll do to me."

"Good point." I transported us down the street. I'd aimed for the other side, but instead landed next to the town tailor. "Okay. I have an idea. I'm going to make myself look like a police officer and go to the scene."

"A uniform can't hide your face, Ab. You think he won't know it's you?"

"Not if I look like someone who's already there."

"But you need something from that person to do that."

"That's why I have you."

"How did I know you were going to say that?"

"I'll make you a bird. You get something from an officer and bring it back to me. Easy."

"Right. Grabbing something with a beak and claws is no

problem. No one will notice a thing. And what're you going to do with this person while you're impersonating him or her? Send them to never never land?"

"I'm a powerful witch. He won't even know what hit him." I swirled my finger and tapped him on the nose.

Cooper transformed into a crow. He cawed and flew off. I leaned against the wall of the Holiday Hills Tailor Shop and waited. The city shut down completely at night. The moon lit the night sky, but darkness surrounded the sidewalk and stores. A chilly breeze skirted past. I rubbed my arms to stay warm. "Come on Coop," I whispered.

A barn owl in the distance hooted, "Who cooks for you?"

I rubbed my hands together.

A shadow flew just above the street. Was it a witch? A warlock? Something worse? I moved to the side and pressed my back against the shops window at the corner of the building. Whatever it was, I didn't want it to see me. I turned and glanced down the alley, but it was too dark to see clearly. I smelled rotting eggs. It must have been a dumpster. Something metal crashed to the ground, and a large wolf-like animal climbed to the top of the building and disappeared as the metal object rolled down the alley toward me. I jumped into the air and whipped my hands at the thing to make it stop. When I landed back onto the sidewalk, I conjured a flashlight and shined it into the alley. A silver garbage can lay on its side. I aimed the flashlight at it then at the roof of the tailor, but whatever I had seen was gone. My body shivered. I dropped the flashlight and bent down to retrieve it before it rolled into the sewer drain off the sidewalk.

Just then a mouse scurried over and sat on my foot. I screamed. The mouse took off with a squeak. When Cooper landed on my shoulder, I flailed my arms and screamed some more. "No! Get off me!" I twisted, and turned, and jumped as he dug his claws into my skin.

"Abby! It's me! Turn me back!"

I froze. "Oh. Sorry." I twirled my hand and Cooper's familiar face appeared. "I think I saw the killer."

"Give me a second." His eyes rolled in circles. "I'm dizzy." His little head swayed back and forth. "And my stomach hurts." He shook his head and climbed from my shoulder into my arms. "What happened?"

"I saw a wolf-like creature crawl up the side of the building and disappear. I used this flashlight to see, but I dropped it, and then I got spooked by a mouse. When you came back, you just freaked me out more."

He laughed. "A mouse? You, a powerful witch, got spooked by a mouse."

"You're missing the point. I think I saw the killer."

"Did it have horns?"

I leaned back against the wall again. My shoulders sank. "I couldn't tell. It all happened so fast."

"Abby, I'm not saying you're wrong, but werewolves and shifters lurk the streets at night. It could have been anyone."

"It wasn't anyone. It was the killer. I can feel it in my soul. I'm not wrong about this, Cooper."

"I believe you." He handed me a pencil. "Best I could do. Luckily the guy had it stuck between his ear and head."

"Thank you." I held the pencil. "I need to get there more than ever. Do you know who it belongs to?"

"Remmington Sterling."

"Good. He'll understand why I had to do it."

"We can hope. So, what am I doing? I'm not in the mood to hunt mice right now." He climbed out of my arms, fell to the ground, and rubbed his belly. "I've got that stomachache, you know."

"Just have my back and watch for the wolf. I won't be there long." I closed my eyes and gripped the pencil, but before I could even start the spell, Cooper interrupted.

"Hold up. We've got a visitor."

I opened my eyes to Remmington Sterling holding his hand out. "May I have my pencil back, please?" He smiled, glanced down at Cooper and then back at me. "A crow? Really? His claws ripped my shirt."

"I'll pay to have it repaired. I'm sorry." I leaned back on my heels.

"They're just finishing with the scene. I was going to call and warn you, but when a crow showed up out of nowhere and landed on me, I figured you were close."

"Warn me? About what?"

"Martensen was asking about you. He's sending someone to your place to make sure you're home."

"Does he think I killed Deanna?"

"He's leaning that direction. You found Cornelius. He arrested Constance, and then someone murders another committee member. He's connecting the dots in his head, and they're drawing a picture of you."

"I didn't kill either of them."

"I know you didn't. Now, you'd better get home. You don't want any problems for yourself."

"Wait. I think I saw the killer just a minute ago."

He placed his hand on his weapon. "Here?"

I pointed to the side of the building. "It was a wolf or something like one. It went up the wall. I lost it after that."

"Did it have the horns?"

"I couldn't tell. It was dark. But it was the killer."

"How do you know?"

"I just do. I can't explain it, but you have to believe me."

"Wolves and shifters skulk this area every night. They lie

in wait to frighten humans. You probably saw one of them and scared it away."

"No, I don't think that's it. Can you just have your people check the area? Please?"

He exhaled. "Fine. I'll get a few magicals from the department out here." He closed his eyes and mumbled something I couldn't understand. Seconds later, three officers, all ones I recognized, appeared.

I repeated what I saw, and they took off to search.

"Thank you," I said. "What happened at the scene?"

"Other than Martensen thinking you're the murderer? We know Constance Ambrosia didn't murder Deanna. Several of us put locking spells on her cell and every exit, and we encased the entire jail with barrier bubbles. She couldn't get out if she tried." He checked his watch. "Abby, you really need to get home."

"I will. I promise. But I need to know what kind of evidence you found. Any footprints or anything?"

"No foot prints. We dusted the fork for prints, but I can already tell you they're not human. Just like the ones on the weapon that killed Cornelius, but the humans won't find anything, as usual."

"What do you think they are?"

"Animal, but other than that, I can't say." He closed his eyes. "Go. They're close."

I hugged him. "Thank you." I grabbed Cooper from the ground and squeezed my eyes shut. "There's no place like home."

* * *

Five minutes later, my doorbell rang as someone beat on my door. Fate or the universe or the powers that be cut me a break. My transporting went off without a hitch, and I'd had time to create the perfect environment for an alibi in just a few minutes.

I shuffled out of my bedroom, already dressed in my jammies with my hair knotted into a bun on the back of my head, hoping to look like I'd been asleep. I used the transformation spell to change Cooper into Stella. I had enough of Stella's things in my home to change half the town, but one Stella was a handful enough. I hoped having two for a few minutes wouldn't upset the natural flow of things.

Cooper's Stella lay on the couch, eyes half open and complaining about loud noises as I opened the door.

I blinked several times and dropped my jaw into an enormous fake yawn that became a real one. "Officers? Oh no, what's happened?"

"Ms. Odell, I'm officer Steven Cantor. Can you tell me how long you've been home this evening?"

I'd met Officer Cantor shortly after he'd taken a position at the department, and prior to Gabe leaving on assignment. A human, he wasn't in the greatest of shape to chase down criminals, but most of the police in town weren't. He acted professional, so maybe he didn't remember meeting.

Cooper's Stella groaned. "What's going on? It's the middle of the night."

The officer blushed. "Stella? Oh, hey. I didn't know you were here."

"Well, now you do, and I'm cranky because you woke me up."

Well played, Coop. Well played.

"Oh, I'm sorry. Something's happened, and we need to know where Miss Odell has been the past few hours."

Cooper's Stella sashayed to the door and leaned against it. She batted her eyelashes. Cooper had Stella nailed to perfection. "She's been here with me."

"Oh, I didn't know you'd planned to come by here after our date."

Their date?

Cooper rolled with it. A smiled lit up Cooper's Stella's face. "I had to tell her all about it, obviously. But honey, we are exhausted. We've been here since..." She smiled. "Whatever time we finished. It went by so fast. I don't recall when it ended."

"At eight," he said. "Right before I got called in to cover for another officer. He got sick on the job."

"Oh, that's awful," she said. "You tell that Deputy Chief if he has questions to go on and call me, okay sweetie? I've been with my bestie. Now, if you don't mind, I really need my beauty sleep." She smiled. "You call as well, okay?"

He blushed. "Yes. I will," he said. He turned on his heels and left.

I slammed the door and returned Cooper to his true cat self. Or the cat self I'd known him as. I wasn't quite sure what self was the original Cooper.

"Dang," he said. "I deserve an Oscar for that performance." He shook his head. "Dude needs a shower. He smelled."

"I was too busy not freaking out to notice."

"Consider yourself lucky."

I fell onto the couch. "Stella was out with Steve Cantor tonight? Why didn't she tell me?"

He climbed onto the couch arm. "Did you see that guy? I wouldn't have told either." He shuddered. "Pretending to be a female is exhausting, but to flirt with a guy like that? I think I might be ill."

I lifted him off the couch and set him on the wood floor just off the carpet. "Not on my couch, please."

I thanked Cooper for the light-hearted reprieve — he

had kidded about being sick — and I thought I could sleep, but I couldn't. I tossed and turned until I finally gave up. I removed a pad of paper from my makeshift desk in my little living room and sat on the couch. I wrote everything I knew about everyone on the committee, then created a timeline for all committee communication and events on the day of Cornelius's murder. I'd required the committee members to CC me on everything, and mostly, I thought they had. Once I had the times and senders down, I realized I'd received an update from Cornelius early in the evening before the committee meeting. He'd said Isaac wanted to discuss adding a special category for the best mum contest because his mums needed superior competitors, but he hadn't discussed it with him, and wouldn't. He wrote he'd been tired of Isaac's bragging about his fertilizer, and Deanna's hounding him about the game. And he apologized for the incident at the Enchanted that morning, but it solidified his reasons for being chosen as the committee head.

"Wait a minute."

Cooper jerked awake next to me. "What? What's wrong?"

"Benedict lied to me. I didn't connect it before, but if they'd agreed to work together, Cornelius would have said so in his email update." I pointed to the list. "Look." I showed him the timeline for the day of Cornelius's murder. "He sent that email an hour before the meeting. He and Benedict didn't come to any agreement."

"That's good," Cooper said after yawning. He closed his eyes, rested his head against my leg, and snored.

Maybe Bessie was wrong about the oath. Maybe it was the Barrington family and not the Carrington family. I set the notepad on the coffee table, kept the pencil, and chewed on it while dragging myself to the kitchen for a cup of coffee.

I prepared my Keurig and tapped the pencil on the counter while it brewed.

All magicals could transform themselves. All of them. Including Isaac. I prepared my coffee, scooped a can of salmon into a bowl and rushed them back to the couch. I held the salmon under Cooper's nose. He loved salmon more than he loved tuna. "Cooper. Smell the salmon?"

His little nose twitched. Suddenly, his eyes popped open. He stared at the salmon then raised his eyes to me. "Am I dead? Is this heaven?"

"It's Holiday Hills." I set the bowl on the table and sipped my coffee. "Isaac was upset about that promotion. I mean, he didn't tell me that, but people knew, and he can transform into anything."

Cooper kept his head in his bowl, and with a mouth full of salmon said, "Including a demonized wolf-like creature with horns."

"Exactly!"

He finished the salmon in record time. He licked his paw and swiped it over his face. "And he's always so sticky sweet. I never trust a guy who's always so happy."

I hadn't thought of that, but it made sense. "I need to verify what Bessie said about the Carrington oath. If she's right, then I think we've found our killer."

"Let's not share that, all right?" Cooper asked. "I don't want the killer finding out."

"You and me both."

16

The next morning, I sent Benedict and Isaac texts asking to meet me at the Enchanted an hour apart. News of Deanna's murder took off faster than a lightning strike through town. Even Stella talked about it.

I faked happy and carefree when every part of me ached with exhaustion and guilt. A growing ball of anxiety grew in the pit of my stomach. It would explode if I didn't find the killer. It wasn't even about the festival anymore. I hadn't heard from the mayor, which I decided meant he wouldn't cancel it, and that was great, but finding a double murderer consumed my thoughts. Except I couldn't discuss it with Stella, and not because of the magical part, but because I needed to escape it, to feel normal, if even for a few minutes, fake or real.

I wiggled my eyebrows. "Maybe Officer Cantor can tell you more about it on your next date."

Her eyes widened. "How did you know?"

"Let's just say the cat's out of the bag." Or body. Cooper sauntered over from the kitchen where I would have bet my life savings he'd scarfed down a can of tuna. He rubbed his head against my leg.

"I was going to tell you about it today. This morning. Then the whole Deanna thing happened, and I forgot. But I'm not going out with him again. Can you believe that happened? That's two of the committee members. I'm worried about you."

"Nice deflection there."

"It wasn't deflecting. I'm genuinely worried about you now."

"Don't be. Seriously. I don't even want to think about it right now. I need you to distract me, please."

"Okay." She bit her bottom lip. "Suddenly that feels like a lot of pressure."

I smiled. "How about you tell me why you won't go out with Steve Cantor again?"

"Fine, but don't judge me. You know I have issues about certain things."

Cooper said, "Bet you a case of tuna it's the stink."

I ignored him. I made a cross over my heart. "No judgment."

She exhaled. "He smells like sweaty feet."

I leaned my head back and laughed. "He does not."

"Told you!" Cooper exclaimed. "Should have bet two cases of tuna."

Again, I ignored him.

She nodded. "On our mother's graves. If I'm lying, I'm dying." She crossed her arms over her chest. "Next time you see him, have yourself a sniff. Trust me. You'll smell it."

"I didn't notice it before." I'd been crying earlier, and my nose was stuffy, but that shouldn't have mattered. Most of my power originally generated from my nose. I should have caught it. "I don't know what's worse, you saying he's got sweaty feet stench, or telling me to sniff them." I shuddered. "I think telling to sniff them wins."

"Imagine spending two hours with the guy." She blanched then swallowed hard. "I can't even think about doing that again."

My phone dinged with a text alert. I left it for that moment. "You might have to. He really likes you."

"How do you know?"

"Because he got called into work after you parted company," I smirked. "And came by my apartment to check my alibi for Deanna's murder."

She gasped. "I knew I should be worried about you! He thinks you killed her? What a jerk." She pushed her chair back. "Let me deal with him."

"No," I said. I pulled her arm and made her sit. "Martensen told him to check. But it's okay. I was home, and he knows I have a good alibi."

She fidgeted in the chair. "I don't care. I'm using that as my excuse to end our budding relationship."

Benedict walked up behind her. "Abby. You wanted to talk with me?"

I wiggled my toes in my boot to release some anxiety. It didn't help.

Stella drank the last of her coffee and hung her bag over her shoulder. "I'm sure you two have a lot to talk about, and I've got to run as it is." She smiled at Benedict. "I'm sorry about Deanna. I know you two were friendly."

As she walked away, I said, "Let's go into the book nook. We'll have some privacy there."

Bessie created a small room off the back of the café bookstore for book clubs to meet and discuss my books. Well, not just my books, but they had been the push for the room. She wanted to promote my writing. I loved her for it, but it wasn't necessary.

I closed the door behind us. When I turned around, Benedict's eyes stabbed me like daggers. "I didn't kill Deanna."

I sat and motioned for him to do the same. "I'm not accusing you of anything, Benedict." I smiled. "But I find it interesting that you went there without even letting me speak."

"Come on, Abby. Of course, that's what you're thinking, or you wouldn't have called me here. What is it then? The festival? I'm sure it's going to be canceled."

My phone dinged again. I checked the message. The mayor had texted twice. "From the tone of the texts I just received from Mayor Howe, I think you're right, but I won't let that happen. It's not that, anyway. I want to talk to you about shifters and werewolves."

His lips formed a thin line. "Okay."

"Did you shift last night?"

"I shift every night, Abby."

"Were you off Main Street by the church?"

His shoulders stiffened. "So, you are blaming me for Deanna's murder." He stood.

"No, I'm not. Please sit."

He sat but scowled at me.

"Deanna called me right before her death. She asked to meet at the church."

"And?"

"And she said she knew who murdered Cornelius."

He pressed his lips together and leaned back in the chair. "Did she say it was me?"

"She only said it was someone from the committee. I got

there too late, but a shadowy figure was there. It ran around the church corner."

"It wasn't me."

"Let me finish, okay?"

He nodded.

"It was on all four legs, and the night of Cornelius's murder, something ran away as well. It was too dark to tell what it was. I thought maybe it was a person running, and they lost their balance because it was bent over, but I'm beginning to think I was wrong."

"It was a werewolf. That's obvious. They don't have a problem going from four legs to two. Wolves can't do that. And we know werewolves have blood cravings."

I wasn't ready to tell him I saw the wolf-like creature near the tailor. "Except Cornelius' and Deanna's murders weren't to satisfy a blood craving. Someone murdered them with garden tools. A werewolf wouldn't need a garden tool for murder."

"Why does any of this matter to you, Abby? I heard Deputy Chief Martensen warning you to stay out of his investigation. Can't you just let the police do their job?"

"It matters to me because two of my committee members are dead, and I don't want anyone else murdered. Benedict, we both know the police can't do their job well when a supernatural being is their criminal."

"The magical ones can."

"And they're working on it, but they're not getting anywhere."

His body relaxed. "Then talk to a werewolf. Seems like that's your best option."

"The wolf-like being that murdered Cornelius and Deanna had horns."

His eyes widened. "What?" He paused and added, "Probably a rabid werewolf then. That happens." He rubbed his eyes. "That's awful. It's just awful."

"It's too bad Cornelius didn't take the time to tell the committee about you two working together. Things would have been much easier for everyone after he died."

He exhaled. "As I said, he had to leave."

"You were the last one at the church that night. Isn't that what you said?"

"I'm always the last one, and yes, I told you that as well."

I approached his lie as an assumption rather than the truth. "What if you and Cornelius hadn't worked things out before the meeting? What if you waited for everyone to leave? What if you waited for Deanna and Cornelius to finish their conversation to approach him? And what if it didn't turn out like you planned, and things got ugly? You could have shifted into anything."

The cords in his neck tightened.

"I saw shoe prints in the mud. I could be wrong, but I think they were sneakers." I glanced at his feet. He'd worn an expensive looking pair of loafers, but that didn't mean he didn't own a pair of sneakers. Didn't everyone? "You could have shifted to human form and left them, then reverted to wolf and took off when you heard me."

"I told you. I didn't kill anyone."

"Cornelius emailed me shortly before the committee meeting. He always sends me a summary update. He mentioned his frustration with Deanna's hounding him and Isaac's request to discuss a special mum category because of his fertilizer. You know what he didn't mention?"

He ran a hand through his dark hair and shook his head. "Fine. We hadn't made that agreement, okay? I lied. There. Now you know. And yes, I tried to talk to him after the meeting, but he refused. He wouldn't listen to anything I had to say. I got mad, and I shifted, but I'm not sick. I'm not some kind of demon, Abby. I don't have horns."

He appeared to be telling the truth, but how could I be sure? "Is that all that happened?"

"That's it. I'll say it again. My story won't change. I had come outside to lock and leave, and I saw Deanna charging away. I knew she was angry, and I knew she'd probably lit up Cornelius as well, but I'd made that list, and I wanted to talk to him about it." He swiped his hand down his face. "Like I said, he wouldn't listen. We argued. I got mad, and I shifted."

"And then what? You left?"

"At first yes, but then I remembered I hadn't locked the back. I'd calmed a bit, so I returned to this form, and as I did, I landed in the mud behind the church. You probably saw my prints back there."

"Then how come I didn't see traces of them on the gravel?"

He dragged his hand down the side of his face. "Because I saw Cornelius fall to the ground. I saw him from underneath the dumpster." He shook his head. "I don't know, I guess I just panicked. I shifted back to my wolf form. Then you showed up, and I didn't know what to do, so when I could, I ran. It wasn't me you saw."

"How do I know it wasn't you?"

"Because I saw it too." He stood.

"Wait," I said. "You saw the wolf-like creature?"

He nodded.

"Why should I believe you? You've already lied to me."

"I just told you I was there. I saw what you saw. Why would I lie?"

I took a breath. "Did you see horns?"

"No. I just saw it running. It was in front of me, running on all fours."

"How am I supposed to believe you?"

"Watch." He closed his eyes, leaned his head back, and raised his arms.

I watched as his body morphed from man to wolf. First his shoes disappeared, and long-nailed, dark gray, furred paws replaced them. Then his pants shredded from his tight muscled wolf legs. Next, his chest and head transformed into his wolf self. My heart raced.

He lifted his head toward the ceiling and howled with enough force to make the table shake.

17

I pushed my back into the chair and held up my hand ready to cast a spell to contain him. "Don't even think about it, Benedict!"

As I began to twirl my hand, he growled. "Wait," he said in a raspy, deep voice. He leaned his head down near me. "No horns." He parted the tuft of hair between his ears. "Not even a marking."

My heartbeat slowed back to normal. I took a deep breath and waited as he shifted back to his human form.

"I didn't mean to scare you. I just wanted you to see. I don't have horns. I can't have horns."

"What do you mean you can't? You can shift into anything."

"No, I can't." He dug into his pocket and removed a silver coin. "Here. This is proof."

He placed the coin in my hand.

"Is this about the oath you took?" I examined what I thought was a coin but was an amulet. I flipped it over and scrutinized it for small lines to check its authenticity. "How am I supposed to believe you've kept that oath?"

"Because I'm telling the truth. Only the town council knows about the oath. How did you find out?"

"Bessie's on the town council. She doesn't believe you killed anyone."

"She's right."

"Benedict, why didn't you tell me any of this before? Why did you lie?"

He sat back in the chair. "Because I wanted the stupid committee head position. I didn't expect to lie. It just came out, and then I couldn't backtrack. I'm sorry Abby. I truly am. Please tell me you believe me."

My gut told me he spoke truth. "I believe you."

He sat back down. "What happens now? Two committee members are dead. Could this be about the festival?"

"I think it's about Cornelius."

"But they murdered Deanna as well."

"Because she knew it was a committee member."

"Damien?"

I shook my head. "The department has cleared him. And me."

"Constance could have escaped jail. The breakup devastated her. Everyone knew she lied about it. Cornelius made sure of that."

"The magicals on the force cast spells to keep her from escaping."

"Then we've only got one choice."

I nodded. "Isaac."

"The promotion. He was so angry about that. You need to tell Martensen."

I shook my head. "He won't believe me. He won't listen to anything I say. I need to get Isaac to confess. Did you talk to him about what happened?"

He nodded. "Like I said, he was upset. He said he told

Cornelius he'd applied for the job and the next thing he knew, Cornelius was on the interview schedule. He went into his interview, and they told him he wasn't being considered because he'd altered his timecard."

"I wonder if he did?"

"He swore he didn't."

"Did Cornelius admit to telling their work?"

"Not that I know of, but Isaac believed it was him. He did it out of spite, he'd said. His human resources manager showed him the altered timecard in the system. They said it was almost impossible to alter, and if he hadn't been dishonest, they would have promoted him because of that skill alone. Cornelius is basic with technology. Isaac said he wasn't qualified for the job."

"So, Cornelius magically altered the timecard and probably cast a spell over human resources to hire him," I said.

"That's exactly what Isaac claimed." He adjusted his shirt collar. "I don't know about you, but that sounds like a motive for murder to me."

"I agree."

"So, what happens now?"

I stared at the wall thinking up a plan. "I need to think about that."

He stood. "If you need help, I'm in. But Abby, be careful."

He walked out of the book club room.

My cell phone rang. I checked the ID and answered the call on speaker. "Mayor Howe," I said. "We are not canceling the festival."

"You don't have a say in that, Abby."

"Yes, I do. It's my festival now, and I guarantee I can get the town to side with me. This festival supports the library. That library is important to the community. If you think they're going to let it close from lack of funding, you don't know your constituents, sir."

"We have two murders. The community needs to be safe. Having a large group of people gathered in one space isn't safe."

"The killer isn't killing with an audience. I just need a little more time. Let me at least get the festival set up. If you decide you really want to cancel after you see the community's response, then fine. I'll agree to canceling. Can you do that for me? For my mother's legacy?"

He sighed through the phone. "I loved your mother. Fine. Set up. We'll assess the community reaction once you complete the set up."

"Thank you! I've got to run. I need to get my committee moving."

"If another murder happens, and Lord, I hope one doesn't, I'm holding you responsible," the mayor said before disconnecting the call without a goodbye.

I tapped an email on my phone announcing Benedict as the new committee head and assured the group they weren't in danger, and they weren't. Not since I knew who the murderer was. I also requested their presence at the church to set up the festival at seven o'clock that night. It was time to take down Isaac Rivers.

* * *

My completed second drafts of my manuscripts were due to my agent. I asked Bessie to cast a concentration spell on me, so I'd get it all done, but she refused. So, I got to work the human way. I tightened and re-tightened my final manuscript for my agent. My heart rate kicked into overdrive as I finished sending the attachments. Despite the tragedy happening around me, I couldn't stop smiling. The manuscripts had been rough, but I'd refined them so much, they'd shined. Perfection. I'd even given them a nose twinkle for a copyedit and proofreading. Magic wasn't a replacement for an editor, but it made their job easier. Personal gain? No. I did it for the editors.

"Abby?"

I glanced up at Constance. "You're out of jail!"

She sat beside me. "Shh. I don't want the world to know they locked me up."

I tilted my head. "This is Holiday Hills, remember? Everyone knows."

She sighed. "True." She leaned closer. "I told the police the truth. That's why they let me out. Deanna's murder is terrible, but it didn't prove my innocence to Martensen." She frowned. "I know you're trying to find the killer. Officer Sterling told me. I want to tell you the truth as well."

"Okay."

"I was trying to convince Cornelius to take me back like I said, though I can't imagine why now. His refusal destroyed me. Had Deanna not interrupted when she did, I don't know what would have happened."

"Is that why you went to a male friend? For comfort?"

"But it wasn't a date. It was a therapist."

"Really? That is not what I expected you to say."

She laughed. "It wasn't what I expected to do, that's for sure. But I didn't trust myself. I've never felt the emotions I felt with Cornelius. Not the love, not the anger, not the pain. I needed to put things in perspective."

"And the police believe you?"

"They talked to the therapist. Yes, I went there magically, but you know how it works. He couldn't say that. I don't know what he told Deputy Chief Martensen, but it worked. I'm sorry I lied to you. I hope you understand why I had to do it."

I did. "It's okay."

"Thank you. I'm glad. Abby, are we safe? Do you think these murders have to do with the festival?"

I bit my bottom lip. "No, and that's why I've convinced the mayor to let us continue with the setup. If all goes as planned, we'll catch the killer."

"That's a risky way to go about it, don't you think?"

"Don't worry." I smiled. "I think I have a plan."

Damien walked into the Enchanted. He smiled and waved when he saw us. He ordered his coffee and walked over while Bessie prepared it. "Ladies." He placed his hand on Constance's shoulder. "I'm glad to see you out and about. I can't believe the police thought you murdered Cornelius."

She smiled up at him. "Thank you for saying that."

He squeezed her shoulder. "Anytime." He made eye contact with me. "I got the email about Benedict. I think that's a great idea. If the festival happens. I've heard talk about it being canceled." Bessie handed him his coffee. "Thank you."

Cooper hopped onto my lap. "What's wrong with men? Don't they ever shower? Dude stinks."

I pressed my lips together.

"Abby?"

I glanced up at Damien. "Oh, sorry I was thinking. No one will cancel the festival. I've already spoken to the mayor. I believe they'll catch the murderer before opening night."

"That's putting a lot of faith in our law enforcement, and without Gabe, I'm not sure it's going to happen. Martensen isn't the brightest bulb in the box."

"He might need a little push."

He raised an eyebrow. "You like wearing your little amateur sleuth hat, don't you?"

"This is for my mother's legacy and the library's funding. It's not about me."

"I'm sure. You know who did it, don't you? You've figured it out."

"No, I haven't figured it out. I'm just hopeful Martensen will soon."

"Not sure that's possible," he said. "I know I pegged the wrong person."

"And that was?" Constance asked.

"Deanna. She was so angry about that game."

"What about Benedict or Isaac?" she asked. "Everyone had issues with Cornelius."

He nodded. "Benedict sure did, and there was that issue at work with Isaac. Something about timecards? But I don't know. I think we need to look at someone out of the circle. Cornelius wasn't a well-liked guy."

"Then what about Deanna?" I asked.

He shrugged. "That one stumps me."

"Me, too," I lied.

18

I spent the rest of the day working on the final layout for the festival and my plan to get Isaac to confess. I added a few extra events including pin the tail on the donkey, which I dedicated to Deanna. I gave the donkey a black witch hat to honor her. It wasn't pin the tail on the witch, but it was close, and that was the best I could do. After I secured my plan, I explained it to Cooper.

He laughed. "You're not serious, are you?"

I glared at him.

"Oh, wow. You are." He climbed onto the table. "He's going to know right away. I have to be honest. This is the stupidest thing you've thought up since the dance party at the roller rink for your ex's birthday."

"I'd prefer we don't talk about my ex-husband. His cheating on me may have been a lifetime ago, but I still don't enjoy thinking about it."

"I'm being serious. If Gabe was here—"

"Gabe's not here, and if he was, we wouldn't be dealing with this. But we are because Martensen can't get anything right."

"What about Sterling? Can't you involve him?"

"I'll call him. I promise."

"Good because you've never worked a job with a computerized timecard. Why would you suddenly want one for a volunteer position? I'm telling you, he's going to know you're setting him up." He stood on his hind legs and squeezed the muscles in his other legs. He sucked in a breath and made his tiny chest stick out. "Hi-ya!" He swung a stiff arm toward my face, but it was too short to reach. "I'll have to get all cat-ninja on him." He lifted a back leg and toppled off the table, landing with a loud, weighted *thunk*. "I'm fine. Landed on all fours."

* * *

I met Phoebe Booth at a small coffee shop in the town over. I hadn't seen her since my mother's celebration of life. She'd moved away, not far, but had moved back for a new job a few months before. A new job where Isaac and Cornelius worked. She returned right before Isaac lost his promotion.

"You understand technology, don't you?" I asked.

She smiled. Her white teeth sparkled so bright I wanted to put on sunglasses. "It's kind of my thing. Why? Do you have a tech issue you need help with?"

I'd ordered an iced tea and added two packets of sugar to my glass. "I need to get a copy of your timecard program at work."

"TWAT?"

I spit my tea out. "I'm sorry?"

"Technological Workplace Annal Test." She smiled. "TWAT. Four men developed it. Go figure. Two while going through divorces. They said it took them six weeks to come up with that." She laughed. "They named it after their ex-wives."

"I don't even know how to respond to that," I said.

"Most brilliant thing I've ever heard," Cooper said.

She pointed at Cooper. "He's your familiar."

"Is it that obvious?" I asked.

"Only because I heard him say the name was brilliant."

My eyes widened. Cooper climbed from my lap onto the table. "You can understand me?"

"I'm a very gifted witch."

"Apparently so," he said. He leaned his head back toward me. "Why can't you do amazing stuff like that?"

I shook my head and looked at Phoebe. "You need a familiar? Mine's free to a good home."

"No thanks. I'm good. I've got a corgi in the car. She's mine."

Cooper laughed. "A corgi? What's she do? Wiggle her butt into bad people's legs and knock them over?" He laughed again but stopped when he felt my eyes burning into him. He nuzzled against me. "Sorry. I'm hangry."

The fact that he knew the word hangry, and that it meant anger caused from hunger didn't surprise me. I called the server over and ordered a tuna salad sandwich, no mayo, no mustard, onion, egg, or celery.

"You should have just asked for a can of tuna," Phoebe said. "So, why the TWAT?"

Cooper laughed again. I patted his back with a little more intensity than normal. "My bad," he said.

"I can't tell you, but I promise it's important."

She stared me in the eye, then nodded. "Done."

"Wow! That was easy."

She shrugged. "Promise you'll tell me when you're done?"

"Oh, you'll know."

She leaned toward me. "Is this about Cornelius Stone's murder?"

I swiped my finger across my lips. "Can't tell you that either."

"I'm going to like this."

An hour later we were back in my car, my laptop set up with TWAT — I couldn't believe they'd named it that — and I knew everything I needed to know about it.

"How do you enter your timecard?"

"Cooper, please. Phoebe explained the system. I don't need to be quizzed."

"You think the tech spell will stick? Like, after we catch Isaac?"

"No."

He groaned and climbed onto my dashboard. "That's too bad."

"I won't have to do anything. I'm just going to ask him to help me with it. He'll see it, panic, and then he'll know I know."

"And try to kill you."

"You heard me on the phone with Remmington Sterling. He's going to have ten magicals staged around the set up. I'll be fine. We'll be fine."

"We'd better be."

* * *

I arrived at the church earlier than the rest of the committee. Remmington dropped by and informed me that he'd stationed men nearby and they'd get into position once the tents went up.

"I'll do that right now," I said. I wanted most everything set up before the committee arrived anyway, and magic was the only way to do it. A flick of the hand and the game section appeared. Another flick and the food court came to life.

"Impressive," Cooper said. "Is there tuna there?"

I smiled down at him. "Second hut on the right. Already in a bowl waiting for you."

"Be right back."

Cooper didn't run much, and his speed always surprised me. I flicked my wrist and created the dunk tank.

Damien jumped from behind it. I hadn't seen him. "Whoa, that was close." He brushed dust and dirt from the parking lot off his sweater and smiled.

"Oh, my gosh! I'm so sorry. I didn't see you there."

"No worries." He nudged his shoulder into mine. "Taking the easy way out, I see."

I smiled. "I call it making sure we get the big stuff done this evening."

He nodded. "Works for me. I'd help but..." He swirled his finger, but nothing happened. "I can shift into a carnival game, but I can't make one appear."

"Have you ever done that? Shifted into an inanimate object?"

"A few times. It's awkward."

"What's awkward?" Benedict asked. He'd walked up and stood next to Damien.

"Shifting into inanimate objects."

Benedict laughed. "That's awful. You feel nothing. Strangest thing I've ever done."

"That's good information. I'll make sure I never turn myself into something inanimate." I smiled. "But it's back to work for me." With that, I twirled my finger and created the fun house.

"Wow," Benedict said. "You're pretty good at this magic thing."

"Did you question it?"

He shook his head. "What do you need me to do?"

"I need the tank filled. The portable toilets — oh, hold on." I gave my wrist a twist and the small plastic bathrooms popped up across from the dunk tank. "I expected that. Can you move them back a little and straighten them into a line after filling the dunk tank?"

Benedict gave me a thumbs up. "Sure thing, boss."

"And you," I said pointing to Damien. "Can you check the fun house? Same things as last year, only this is a different one. It comes with three exits, but I think we should have at least five. But don't make them too obvious. We want the families stressed a little, but not fearing for their lives."

He smiled. "Definitely don't want our guests freaking out. I'm on it." He jogged away.

* * *

Constance arrived right at seven. I assigned her the game section. "Oh, how fun," she said. "I love organizing things."

"Good. If you need help with something, just ask Damien or Benedict. They're here."

"I will." She whispered, "If you need help, I'm here."

I smiled. "Thank you. I've got it covered." I examined the park. Things were coming along, but where was Isaac? Why hadn't he arrived?

saac didn't show up until seven-thirty. "Great! You're
here." I put on my cheerful face and pretended I didn't
think he murdered my friends. "I have a favor."

"What's up?" He stuffed his hands into his jean pockets.

"Do you know Phoebe Booth? I think you work
together?"

His Adam's apple moved up and down. "Yes. Why?"

"Last week I spoke with her about a timecard system,
and she offered to sneak me a copy of the one used at your
work. She showed me how to use it, but I'm a type and print
kind of girl. Technology is not my friend. She said you could
help if I needed it." I slouched my shoulders. "And I need it."

"Why do you need timecards? This is volunteer work.
We shouldn't have to clock in and out."

"A little birdie told me we might get funding from the
town to pay us for our time. You know how much my mom
wanted that for you all. I just thought I'd get a head start
and track time so we could show them the value of it. At
least at the event."

He flinched. "Is this a joke? Because it's not funny."

"A joke? Why would I joke about money?"

"Because." He shook his head. "Forget it."

"Does that mean you'll help?"

"I guess."

Like my character's had done in their books, I had set up my suspect to trap him. My plan almost failed before it started but crossed the finish line in the last second. "Isaac, have I said something that's upset you?"

He pressed his lips together, paused, then shook his head. "You know what happened at my work, right?"

I smiled. "Your promotion. You told me. I think that's amazing!"

His brown eyes darkened. "I didn't get the promotion because I earned it, Abby. I got it because of Cornelius's murder."

I feigned surprise by dropping my jaw and shaking my head. "What do you mean?"

He moved to stand beside me, giving himself a clear view of the parking lot turned festival in front of us. "Cornelius and I applied for the job. During his interview he told human resources I'd been clocking in and out from home, and not working the hours I claimed."

"You mean like skipping work?"

"No. They'd know that. Just adding an hour a day. I don't know how he did it, but he showed them I'd digitally altered the system. So, during my interview, which turned out to be an interrogation, they confronted me about it." He pinched the bridge of his nose. "Cornelius got the job because of it. He didn't even have any experience in the department. I've been in it for ten years. The job should have been mine."

"Did you manipulate the system?"

He turned and glared at me. "What? No. I could have,

but I didn't. Why would I do that for an extra five hours a week?"

I shrugged. "Twenty-five a month sounds like a lot."

"I didn't do it, and now that I've got the job, I'm kicking butt, but I know they're just waiting until they can find someone to replace me." He kicked a rock. "I'm not a thief, and digitally altering my timecard is stealing money from the company."

"I'm sorry you had to deal with that. Had I known, I wouldn't have asked for the program."

"It's just a reminder of how Cornelius screwed me over, and that's not even the worst of it. Someone told Deputy Chief Martensen. He told me not to leave town."

"Was this recently?"

He nodded. "This afternoon. I guess they think I killed Cornelius and Deanna. I've got an attorney, but I hope it doesn't go that far."

"All because of the timecard thing? What would that have to do with Deanna?"

He shrugged. "I have no idea."

"Do you have an alibi for the time she died?"

"Not really. I was at work, but no one else was there. Just like the night Cornelius died."

"But you have the timecard to verify that, right?"

He laughed. "They'll talked to HR. That won't help."

"I can't believe Martensen would think you or anyone from the committee, can do such horrible things."

He stared down at his foot, moving it back and forth in the gravel and coating the leather with dust. "Right, but it is what it is. Let's get on that program."

"Fantastic. Can you show everyone how to punch in?"

"Sure." He laughed. "Can you believe they named it TWAT?"

Heat climbed up my neck. I turned away when it reached my cheeks. "Don't get me started on that."

* * *

The power going to the ticket booth blew. I jogged over to the electrical box on the side of the church and flipped switches then peeked around the corner to see if Constance, who helped, gave me a thumbs up or down.

After four downs, I finally got it right. I jogged back over, meeting Damien on the way.

"What's next?" he asked.

"Candace said she couldn't get the deep fryer working. Can you check on it?"

"Can't you just do that twirling hand thing?"

"If you can't fix it."

"Got it." He swiveled around and headed toward the food area.

Back at the ticket booth, Constance had wrapped her sweater around her waist, leaving her arms dangling in the breeze. "How's things going?" she asked.

"Okay. We're getting close to being done for the night." I pointed up at the lights we'd spread around the parking lot. "Do you think we need more light? I don't want anyone scared of the shadows."

"It's a fall themed festival. We've got scary stuff all over."

I pressed a finger to my lips. "Maybe we should get rid of that and just make it all mums?"

Isaac showed up. "How's it going?"

"Good," I said. "Did you get everyone to clock in?"

He nodded. "Wasn't hard. Damien helped me explain it. So, what's next?"

"Oh!" I made a fist and pumped it into the air. "The mums! We need the category signs hung on the tables." I pointed to the box on the ground next to the ticket booth.

"There are pins and tape in there. Can you make it look pretty?"

Constance laughed. "I'll help. Men and pretty don't mesh."

"Thank you!"

"Can we make an additional category for ones with specialized fertilizer?" Isaac asked.

"Go for it," I said. I doubted he'd be out of jail in time to compete anyway. I leaned against the ticket booth and watched them walk away. Isaac had placed his hand on the small of Constance's back. Every few steps he moved a little closer to her. Maybe the murders weren't about work after all? Maybe Isaac had fallen victim to Constance's enchanting charm? Could he have murdered Cornelius so she would notice him?

Damien bumped his shoulder into mine. I jerked backward. "You scared me!"

He flicked his head toward Isaac and Constance. "Think it's a love connection?"

"You know, I was just wondering about that."

"I hope not. That woman's the best enchantress I've ever known. She's got us all under her trance."

"She didn't have Cornelius under it," I said.

"Oh, she did."

"You think? Why would he break up with her then?"

"Maybe he realized the competition was too fierce? He knew she wouldn't stay with him forever."

"Strange. Cornelius was always so confident. Overly so most of the time."

"Men of all species fake their true feelings. It's how we get things done." He tucked his hands into his jacket pockets. "Where're they going?"

"To finish the category tables."

He nodded. "Got anything left to do?"

I glanced around the park. We'd all done so much in so little time, especially Damien. The fun house required physical and mental work, and he'd spent a large amount of his time getting it right. I was both proud and impressed. "I think you deserve a break. You've worked hard." I bent around the side of the booth and opened a cooler. "Beer or soda?"

"Beer, please."

I handed it to him and retrieved a soda for myself. "Have you seen Cooper at all? He's been MIA most of the night."

"Did you feed him?"

I giggled. "I did. How did you know?"

He smiled. "I saw him dragging himself into the fun house. I told him to leave, but he laid down and fell asleep in like, seconds."

"That's his gift." I set down my soda can. "Wish me luck. I'm going in."

"I'm headed to break up a one-sided, doomed love connection. We don't want another guy wrapped up in her spell. It's impossible to break."

20

I hadn't exaggerated when I said Damien did a great job on the fun house. I stood at the entrance and hollered for Cooper. I called for him three times, but he didn't appear. "Great," I said to no one. "I so don't want to go in there."

I hated fun houses. Always had. Always would. I had walked through a haunted house before I knew of my heritage, but since discovering my witchy powers, I'd realized many of the tricks I'd seen in haunted houses weren't tricks at all. They were real hauntings. Nope. Not for me.

Fun houses weren't much different, except their scare factor sat at maybe a level two, while a haunted house passed ten.

"Cooper? Come on. I need you." That was a lie, but familiars were supposed to come when called. I leaned my head back and sighed. "I'm so feeding you canned cat food for this." I stepped into the fun house and the music blasted to life, forcing me to cover my ears. Mirrors lined the walls. I saw myself in five ahead of me, but I couldn't judge the distance between them because of their warped design. I stretched out my arms and hit one. I moved to the right and hit another. "Cooper!" I stepped to the left and found an opening. I kept my arms stretched for fear I'd run into a trick.

"Cooper! Where are you?" I kept moving, walking through a small room filled with balls I had to climb through, another room with ladders draped from one side to the other. I stuck my foot in mud underneath one and water under another one until I found the right ladder. "Great. I love these boots. Cooper!"

Three doors enclosed me into a small space. My heart rate zoomed into dangerous territory. My throat dried. I struggled to breathe. Pick a door! Pick a door!

I yanked on the first handle, but it wouldn't budge. The second didn't either. "Seriously?" I pulled on it again, and it gave. I wrenched it open and ran through it. The lights flashed on, then a disco ball came to life, swirling bright colors all over the small room. I froze.

Clowns. I closed my eyes and dragged my hand down my face. "It's not real, Abby. It's not real." My body shook. My teeth chattered. The air was so thick I couldn't breathe. "It's not real!" I couldn't convince myself of that, so I focused on the front entrance. I needed out, and pronto.

The music and lights stopped. I waited a moment before opening my eyes. I didn't want it to be a trick. I inched one eye open. The lights flashed back to life, and the music screamed on. Tears pooled in my eyes. "Cooper!"

Why was I panicking? Fake clowns couldn't hurt me. The music blared so loud I couldn't think. I had to focus. I had to shut it out. I swirled my hand, but nothing changed. I squeezed it into a fist. "Work!" When I twirled it again, the clowns moved toward me.

I backed into the wall. "No. No. No. No." I flicked my wrist and squeezed my eyes shut. "Make them stop!"

The music and lights shut down. The air lightened. My lungs relaxed a little, but I still hadn't opened my eyes. I needed my heart to stop racing first Something wasn't right. No cool breeze broke its sail against me. No sounds from my committee members even moving. Everything stayed still and silent. I must have transported myself into another room. I opened my eyes and screamed.

I fell to the ground and crawled back against the wall. I hadn't escaped. The clowns stood looming over me like skyscrapers in the sky. One leaned over me, barely inches from my face. The mountain man. Only, it wasn't Gabe. Up close I saw different eyes. Dark, evil eyes. I covered mine with my arm and tucked my head down. "Leave me alone!"

"Gabe's not coming home."

I patted the floor hoping to find something to throw at him. "Shut up! Shut up!"

"Gabe's not coming home."

"Leave me alone!" I screamed that over and over until my throat was too raw to swallow.

The music and lights stopped. "Abby? Is that you?"

I slid down onto my right side, my breathing shallow, body shaking, and throat so dry and sore I could only whisper. "Over here."

Damien stared down at me with a flashlight beaming into my eyes. "Are you okay?"

I squinted. "Did you turn off the lights?"

He held up a small black box. "I killed all the power. It's easier to get out that way." He wiggled the flashlight. "This baby can light up a room. It's got five C batteries in it. It's heavy and a pain to carry around, but it works great. Did you find Cooper?"

I shook my head and laughed. It hurt my throat, but I kept laughing, harder and harder. That was what I did to release anxiety, I laughed.

Damien crouched down and helped me up. He laughed too. "What's so funny?"

Once upright, I took a few breaths, counted to five, and then released them. "I'm fine." I fell backwards.

Damien grabbed me before I hit the wall. "You sure you're all right?"

I stared down at my boot. I'd broken the heel. "Oh, great. First creepy clowns, and now a broken heel. I think that muddy ladder room weakened it." I noticed the mud on his sneakers, looked up at him, then back at his sneakers.

Sneakers.

A dried mud line coated a frame around the lower half of his shoe.

It all rolled through my brain like a movie. Damien cozying up next to Constance. Constance all but dismissing him. Suggesting Deanna murdered Cornelius. The shelter's computer check-in system. Damien helping Isaac with the timecard program.

It was Damien? Damien murdered Cornelius and Deanna? He must have figured out how to cheat the time-card system. I pretended not to notice his shoes and frowned when I looked back at him. "These boots were expensive. Hey, speaking of money, did Isaac show you how to check in on that timecard program?"

"You mean TWAT?" He laughed. "We've got that at the shelter. The guys who created it donated it."

I swallowed. He stared at me and took a step closer. "Abby? Are you okay?"

"It was you, wasn't it?"

He stepped closer. "Listen, you have to understand. I—"

I pushed him away and ran. I darted through the door, swung open another one and raced through it. I didn't know where I was or where I was going, but I couldn't stop, or Damien would catch me.

"Abby, you can't keep running."

The lights and music switched on. My head spun. I tasted bile. Keep running! I hit a wall, bounced back, and fell to the ground. I flipped my head around. The door to the room opened. I crawled to my knees and pushed myself off the ground. I yanked another door, but it wouldn't open. My heart raced along with the flashing lights.

"Abby. This is ridiculous. Let's talk. I won't hurt you."

None of the doors worked. I turned around and pressed my body against a door. "Is that what you told Deanna before you stuck that fork into her chest?"

He stopped a foot in front of me.

Focus Abby. Calm yourself. You can't perform magic when you're emotional.

"I didn't want to kill her, but I had to. She knew my secret. I couldn't let her tell anyone now, could I?"

"Cooper," I whispered. "Where are you?"

Damien laughed. "That cat's not coming. I put a little something in that tuna you gave him. He's passed out behind the games." His fingers shifted into dark claws with long, pointy nails. "Constance needed my help." He shook his head, then shut off the disco lights, leaving on only a small light on the ceiling . He hit another button and lowered the music. "She always needs my help, but she never says thank you. All she wanted was that stuck up old warlock. Can't have him now though, can she?"

"That's it, isn't it? You murdered Cornelius because you want Constance. And you killed Deanna because she knew what you'd done."

He laughed again. He held the power box in his hand and clicked a switch. The room went pitch black. He shined his flashlight into my eyes. I flinched and covered them, leaving a small area uncovered for me to see him.

"Deanna was unfortunate. She left me no choice. She thought her fake, human magic would protect her. And believing she could tell me how and why I murdered Cornelius, and I would just turn myself in?" He shook his head. "What a surprise it must have been, the fork stabbing deep into her chest."

"Since we're talking about surprises." I raised my right knee and kicked my foot out with every ounce of strength I could muster. My good boot's heel made powerful contact right where the sun didn't shine. Damien cried out and dropped the power box and flashlight as he bent over. His pants ripped as his wolf body formed beneath them.

He tried to reach for the flashlight. I kicked him in the shoulder. He collapsed onto the opposite side. Shouting in pain, he rolled into a ball, holding his knees up to his chest. He stopped shifting, staying somewhere between wolf and man.

I grabbed the flashlight and held it tight in my hand just as he stretched his legs toward me. He smacked his sneakers into my ankles and knocked me off balance. I fell to the ground, but I kept the flashlight in my hand. I rolled to the left, though it didn't matter.

Damien flung himself on top of me. He grabbed my arm and shook it. "Drop it!" He screamed.

I whipped my arm back and forth, trying to shake his grip loose. "Let go of me!"

"Drop it! You can't overpower me!" He dug his claws into my wrist. "Gabe!" I screamed. "I need you!"

"Stop fighting me!" He tightened his hand around my arm. Pain shot up my arm and into my neck.

I raised my free hand and latched onto his ear to pull him to the side. But it wasn't an ear I grabbed. It was a horn.

He yanked his head to the opposite side and released his grip on my other arm. Just as I raised the flashlight to hit him in the head, a loud growl, the likes of I'd never heard before, bellowed over the music.

Damien's eyes bulged. He let go of me and leaned his head back and howled. I pushed him off me and rolled away. He collapsed to the ground. The growl subsided. I kicked his leg, but he didn't move. I kicked it again just in case, then shined the flashlight on the ground, looking for the power box. I grabbed it and hit five buttons on the thing until the overhead light turned on.

Cooper sat on top of Damien's shoulder licking his paw. "Hey, how's it going?"

I sat back against the wall, breathless. "Where have you been?"

He climbed off Damien, walked a circle around him, and sniffed. "He smells like rotten eggs." He climbed over Damien's chest and smelled his hand. Damien didn't budge. He hissed. "Shine that thing over here, will ya?"

I aimed the flashlight at Damien's clawed hand as it morphed back to human.

Cooper examined Damien's nails, then leaned in close and sniffed them. He blanched and hurried to me. "That's the smell from when we found Cornelius. It looks like dirt in his fingernails."

"I thought that was Isaac's fertilizer."

He shook his head and climbed onto my legs. "Looks like you were wrong about a few things."

"Don't start. I have a headache."

"I'll cut you some slack. By the way, I think your friend here put something in my tuna. One minute I'm eating, and the next I'm waking up from a serious tuna coma. And I didn't even finish the can."

Remmington Sterling burst through the door, gun aimed and ready to fire. "Abby!" He pointed the weapon at Damien. Two other off-duty magical officers followed behind him. "Cuff that one," he said and rushed to me. "Are you okay?"

I nodded. I set the power box and flashlight down. "I need to get up."

He squatted down and held out his hand. "Let me help you."

"No. I've got it. I'm fine." I pressed my hand onto the ground and clipped a button on the power box.

An invisible door swung open, and a clown popped out. It screamed, "Gotcha!"

I grabbed Remmington and pulled him close. "I hate clowns!"

He laughed, his breath touching my face. "So do I."

* * *

Officer Sterling insisted I let the ambulance take me to the hospital. Cooper rode along then snuck into the emergency room and climbed onto my examination bed. When the doctor came in, he saw him and smiled. "Is he your service cat?"

Cooper raised his head. "Service cat? Really? More like hero cat."

I smiled. "Something like that."

The doctor cleared me, saying I'd have a few bumps and bruises, but I didn't need to stay overnight. I called Bessie for a ride home.

"You sure you don't want to transport us there?" Cooper asked.

"I'm too tired to try."

"Probably best."

I didn't even have the energy to tell Bessie what happened. Cooper gave her his limited version, expanding his heroism part with details I didn't recall. I would have argued, but my couch was too comfy, and I couldn't keep my eyes open.

* * *

"Abby. Abby, wake up."

I pulled a pillow from underneath my head and covered my face. "Not now, Coop. I'm sleeping."

"Abby, it's me."

My eyes popped open. I hurled the pillow off my face and across the small room. "Gabe?" I sat up. "You're here!"

I threw my arms up and wrapped them around him. He squeezed me tight as tears slid down my cheeks. "You're here! I can't believe it!"

He kissed the side of my head and released our hug. "Ab, I can't stay."

"What?" I tucked my legs under and pushed my back against the couch. "What do you mean you can't stay?"

He sat on my coffee table. He rubbed his growing beard. "It's going to be awhile. Things are worse than we thought."

"But it's been so long. Can't you get a vacation or something?"

He smiled. "I wish." He leaned in close and brushed the hair from the side of my face. "I need you to stop worrying about me. Live your life, Abby. I don't know when I'll be coming back."

I switched positions, pulling my knees close to my chest

and wrapping my arms around them. I needed protection from his words. "I don't understand."

"Yes, you do. You need to move on. I can't promise you anything right now, and I don't want you pausing your life waiting for me. Please, Abby. Listen to what I'm saying."

"I'm not pausing my life." I dug my nails into the sides of my arms. "I just caught a murderer. That's not pausing my life. Do you think I could just forget about you or something? Like I've never loved you? Is that what you think? Are you here to let me down easily?"

He closed his eyes and opened them as he exhaled. "My feelings haven't changed." He moved over to the couch and leaned his shoulder against its back. "Abby, I need you to hear me, okay? I'm trying to protect you."

I turned toward him. "Protect me from what? I know you're not the mountain man. I saw his eyes."

"It's complicated, but I'll stop him, and when I do, I'll come back. For now, I need you to disassociate with me. It's the only way we can make it through this."

"Wait. What can the mountain man do to me? Am I in danger?"

"He'll use you to get to me. I can't let that happen."

"I can handle him, Gabe. You know that."

He shook his head. "He's stronger than you think. I can't take that risk."

"Why does he want to hurt you?"

He leaned his forehead into mine. "I can't tell you anything more. I just need you to forget about me for now. Please."

"I couldn't do that even if I tried."

"There's a way."

My eyes widened. "No. No. You're not casting a spell over

me!" I shook my head. "I won't let you do that. I won't." Tears fell down my face. I cried into my hands. "I won't!"

He moved my hands and pulled my face to his. He kissed me. I threw my arms around him and kissed him back, feeling all the things I'd missed. The excitement flooding my veins and pumping through my body. The warmth settling in my stomach. The sense of home over-whelming me. He tried to pull back, but I wouldn't let him, and he surrendered into more kissing until I couldn't breathe.

He wiped the tears from my eyes. "I'm sorry, babe."

21

E xhaustion overwhelmed me the next day. Just staying awake for a few minutes wore me out all over again. I slept on and off. Stella visited and brought food. I fell asleep on her while she talked about a new guy she'd met through a dating app. Bessie brought food as well, including cans of tuna, salmon, and sardines for Cooper. I made him eat the sardines on the windowsill. I fell asleep on Bessie too. I apologized each time I saw them, telling them I was just too exhausted to stay awake, but they didn't mind.

I believed the exhaustion was partly because of what happened with Damien, but mostly, it was what happened with Gabe.

The rest of my committee visited me on the second day, late in the afternoon. "Is everything finished?" I asked.

Constance nodded. "We're all good for Friday night. It's going to be fantastic!"

Benedict smiled. "Isaac made two banners to honor Cornelius and Deanna. Oh, and one for your mother, of course."

I smiled at Isaac. "That's great." I reached my hand to his. "I'm so sorry."

He squeezed my hand. "Bessie told me everything. I don't blame you. I would have suspected me as well."

"Are you okay?" Constance asked.

"A little sore, and exhausted, which is weird, but otherwise, I'm fine."

Benedict stood. "We'll let you sleep then. I hope you can be there for the competition Friday."

"You mean to see me win the competition Friday," Isaac said. "That fertilizer is going to blow the other mum's out of the way and win."

"Not if the judges get a whiff," Benedict said.

Isaac laughed. "It smells bad, but I can't help that. I used rotten eggs."

Cooper heard that from the corner of the room. "I knew that's what it was."

"Isaac, did you give Damien any of your fertilizer?"

"No. Why?"

"I smelled it the night of Cornelius's murder. I just didn't know that's what it was."

"Really? I gave Cornelius a bag of it that night. I wanted him to experiment with it, so he'd make the special category."

"There wasn't a bag of fertilizer near him," I said. "Damien must have taken it."

Isaac's smile faded. "He'll never get to use it, so at least there's that."

I yawned. "I'm so tired. What's going on with Damien? I haven't heard, and I'm not reading the paper."

Both Isaac and Constance stood. All three shared a look.

Benedict said, "Bessie hasn't told you?"

I tilted my head to the side. "Told me what?"

Constance blurted out. "Damien's dead."

"Dead? How? What happened?"

"He was sick," Benedict said. "A parasite in his brain. The doctor thinks that's what caused him to grow horns."

I leaned back into the couch. "So, he didn't do this of his own free will?"

"Abby," Constance said. She sat next to me. "Damien decided. He decided not to get help. Don't you question what happened."

"He knew he was sick," Benedict said. "Shifters sense when their health is bad, and with that kind of parasite, he would have sensed it long before it overtook him. He knew what he was doing, and he let it happen."

I didn't know what to say to that, but I was so tired again, I needed to lie down. "I think I need to sleep again. I'll be fine by tomorrow, so Friday won't be an issue, even if I have to cast a spell for it to happen."

"One spell on you is enough," Cooper said.

"What's that supposed to mean?" I asked.

Constance smiled. "Let's let her be. Cooper can take care of her."

When they left, I asked Cooper to explain what he meant.

He climbed onto the coffee table. "You don't remember, do you?"

"I remember everything. No one cast a spell on me."

"What happened after Bessie dropped us off from the hospital?"

"I fell asleep on the couch."

"And then what?"

"I woke up to you hounding me for breakfast."

"And?"

"And what? What are you trying to tell me? What's going on?"

"Nothing," he said. "Nothing at all."

* * *

I slept through Thursday again, but by that night, I'd felt human, or normal. Friday morning came, and I'd never felt better. I showered, put on some makeup for a change, even styled my hair. I dressed in black leggings and a forest green sweater, slipped into my trusted and true knee-length boots knowing their heels wouldn't break, then sprayed a bit of perfume onto my neck.

Cooper jumped off my bed and dry heaved.

I stared down at him. "Oh, the drama."

He sneezed. "It's not drama. I'm allergic to lavender, and that stuff's full of it."

"Really? I didn't know that." I twirled my hand in the air. The scent disappeared. "Better?"

He sniffed the air. "Better. Try the bottle shaped like a woman. I think he'll like that."

I had grabbed a pair of loop earrings, but stopped before putting one in. "Who will like it?"

"Remmington Sterling. I think he's got a thing for you."

"He does not." I pursed my lips. "Does he?"

He jumped back onto my bed. "He's a man. I'm a man, sort of. I know these things."

I shook my head and put on an earring. "He was just helping me out."

"Because he's got a thing for you."

I watched in the mirror as the red swept up my neck to my cheeks. "Stop it." I finished with the other earring and gathered my things to head down to the Enchanted. "Let's go." I opened the door. "You first, you little troublemaker."

"I said what I said," he said and raced down the stairs.

22

"Here, sweetie." Bessie removed my laptop bag from my shoulder. "Let me put this at the table for you." She stepped back and gave me a once over. "Did you get any sleep?"

Cooper skirted between my legs and over to our table. He climbed up to devour a bowl of tuna waiting for him.

I smiled. "I slept like the dead. Stop worrying." I gave her a hug and snuck back my bag. "I'm fine. I promise." I swung my bag over my shoulder, whipped my long hair back as I turned my head and smiled at Mr. Hastings, Mr. Calloway, and Mr. Jameson. "Good morning, gentleman."

They all stared at me with their heads hitched to the side.

Bessie waggled her finger at them. "The polite thing to do is say good morning in return, you old coots."

"Good morning," Mr. Hastings grumbled.

"Oh, yeah. Me too," Mr. Calloway said.

"Hey Abby," Mr. Jameson said. "We heard what happened. Feel like telling us about it?"

I pressed my finger to my chin and grinned. "You know, I think I'll leave that one up to the imagination." I winked.

They're mouths dropped.

I smiled and gave them a little wave. "Have a glorious morning, fellas," I said as I sashayed over to my table.

Mr. Charming flew and landed on Mr. Hastings chair. "What doing Kisses?"

Mr. Hastings leaned away from Mr. Charming. "Get away from me, bird."

Mr. Charming climbed down the chair and wobbled to his perch saying, cantankerous old coot, cantankerous old coot, the entire way.

Bessie covered her mouth to hide her laugh. "I'll get you some coffee." She disappeared into the kitchen.

Cooper moaned as he ate his breakfast. I giggled. "It's so cute when you do that."

He lifted his head up and stared at me. "Excuse me?"

I wiped a little scrap of tuna off his whisker. "Your little food-loving moans are cute."

Bessie returned with my coffee and set it on the table away from Cooper's tail. "Are his moans getting under your skin again?"

"Not at all. I love them. They're adorable." I opened my bag and set my laptop on the table. "Coop, don't get tuna on that, please."

Cooper glanced up at me, shook his head and looked at Bessie. "I think the doctor got it wrong. She's got a concussion."

"I do not. Can't a girl be in a good mood? We caught the person who murdered Cornelius and Deanna, and the mum festival will go on. I can't wait for the flower competition tonight. It's nice to feel happy and excited about something."

Bessie crossed her arms over her chest. "Did you hear from Gabe?"

Cooper coughed. "Excuse me." He jumped off the table. "Hairball." He sprinted behind a row of books.

I shook my head. "Gabe? Nope."

Bessie studied me. "What's going on?"

I sat down and opened an email from my agents. I read it out loud. "My books officially sold! I guess I'm not going to self-publish anymore after all."

Bessie sat beside me. "Abby, you can't avoid this. What's going on?"

Stella burst through the door. "I'm here!" Her cheerful, loud voice caused Mr. Hastings to throw his coffee in the air.

"Bessie!"

"Oh, goodness," Bessie said. She waved her hand, and the mess disappeared.

Stella saw nothing. She pulled out a chair and sat. "So, how's our patient feeling?"

"Perfect. Totally rested and ready for the festival." I pivoted my laptop toward her. "And the deal is done. My current books and a contract for five more."

"That's fantastic!" She opened her bag and removed a small envelope with a note card in it. "Look what I got!"

I smiled. "A tiny note card with no postage?"

"It's from a dozen roses, you mood killer."

"My bad." I opened the note card and read it out loud. "Stella, thank you for two amazing dates. I haven't had that much fun in years. I look forward to showing you off at the festival tonight. Love, Brendan." I held up the note. "Who's Brendan?"

"He's the guy I told you about when you were in dazed and confused mode. Remember?"

"A little, but I was exhausted."

"You'll get to meet him tonight. He's a great guy."

The doors opened. Officer Sterling and Officer Cantor walked in.

"Cantor's here," I mumbled through partially opened lips.

She sighed. "I'll finish later."

They approached the table.

"Coffees?" Bessie asked.

"That would be great," Officer Sterling said. He smiled at me. "How're you feeling? I was going to come by yesterday, but Bessie said you'd been sleeping a lot. I didn't want to disturb you."

"I'm great! How are you?"

Steve inched closer to Stella. She scooted her chair the opposite direction.

Officer Sterling raised his eyebrows and whispered, "She's not interested, is she?"

I shook my head.

He pointed to an empty table across from the fireplace. "Can we talk privately?"

I stood. "Absolutely. I have something to say to you, anyway."

Cooper came from behind and sauntered to the table ahead of us. He climbed onto the top and laid down. "That table over there is too hard. This table is just right."

I ignored him. "Officer Sterling, I just want to thank you again for what you did. I hope you didn't get in any trouble with Deputy Chief Martensen."

"You've only called me Remmington once. That night. That's the only time you've called me by my first name."

I angled my head. "Okay?"

"Abby." He smiled and laughed. "Are you going to make me say it?"

I crossed my arms. "Say what?"

He sighed. "I guess you are. I like you, Abby."

Cooper meowed rather loud. "I knew it!"

I glared at him.

Officer Sterling laughed and turned toward my cat. "Thanks for lightening the mood, Coop." He turned back to me and grabbed my hand. My heart beat faster. "I like you a lot. I don't know what's going on with you and Chief Ryder, but if things are over, and you'd be willing, I'd like to take you to the festival tonight."

"Aw," Cooper said. He rolled onto his back and stuck his legs in the air. "He's so old fashioned. That's adorable."

I narrowed my eyes at him. "Hush," I said.

Officer Sterling smiled. "Is he mocking me?"

I laughed. "A little. He likes that you're old fashioned." I pressed my free hand to my chest. "And I do too."

His eyes widened. "Does that mean you'll go?"

I felt eyes burning into my back. "Bessie and Stella are watching us, aren't they?"

He nodded. "And the parrot." His smile faded. "You're not still with Gabe, are you?"

"Gabe and I aren't together anymore, and I'd love to go with you to the festival, Remmington."

He blinked and dragged his hand down his face. "That's awesome. I've got to sign some papers tonight, but I'll finish about six. May I pick you up at six-thirty?"

"If Martensen lets you go on time, I'll be ready."

He looked over at Stella and Bessie. "They didn't tell you about him, did they? Did they tell you about Damien?"

I exhaled. "I know about Damien. Is Deputy Chief Martensen okay?"

"If you don't count the damage to his ego, yeah. The mayor knocked him down to shift commander. He said he was the worst stand-in chief he's ever met, and a horrible deputy chief too."

My jaw dropped. A flood of relief washed over me. "I hate how that makes me happy, but I don't like him. I hope the next stand-in chief is decent." I whispered, "And magical."

"He's not a stand in. He's the new chief. I think you'll be pretty happy with the mayor's choice."

"Who is it?"

"He'll announce it during his opening speech at the festival. You've got to wait until then." He pulled a card from his pocket. "Here's my cell. If you need to get there earlier, let me know."

23

Cooper raced back to our regular table and meowed his little head off. I waited until Remmington and Officer Cantor left before I said anything.

Stella didn't give me a chance. She grabbed my arm when the door shut. "Okay, that looked mighty intimate. Tell us."

"It's nothing."

Cooper meowed. "Remmington and Abby sitting in a tree. K-i-s-s-i-n-g."

"Remmington and Abby. Remmington and Abby. Kisses," Mr. Charming said.

I booped the bird's nose. "We have not kissed." I smiled. "Yet. We're just going on a date."

"What?" Stella said. "What about Gabe?"

"Yes," Bessie said. "What about Gabe?"

"Gabe's not coming home."

Stella gasped. "How do you know? Is this about that silly dream?"

I shook my head. "It's just a feeling. But it doesn't matter.

I've let go. I can't live my life waiting around for someone who loves his work more than he loves me."

"Wow. I'm in shock."

"She shouldn't be," Cooper said.

"Abby, are you sure this is what you want?" Bessie asked. "You love Gabe."

I shook my head. "I love him, but I'm not in love with him anymore."

"When did this happen?" Stella asked. "Just the other day you were all worried about him."

"I think it's been happening over time, you know, since he's been gone. I don't know, I just woke up the other morning, and I felt at peace. Tired. No, exhausted, but at peace."

Stella just stared at me. "Unbelievable. I'm at a loss for words for the first time in my life." A train horn blew in her bag. "That's my alarm. I have to go. Editing session with a new paranormal author. Lord help me." She grabbed her things and hugged me. "We're not finished talking."

"I'll see you tonight. Maybe we can hang out together."

Bessie pulled the chair beside me close.

Mr. Charming perched onto its back. "What doing?"

Cooper sat on the edge of the table. They all pinned their eyes on me.

"What?"

"Did something happen with Gabe?" Bessie asked.

"You have no idea," Cooper said.

I furrowed my brow. "I called for him when Damien and I were fighting. He didn't come. He promised me he'd always come, but he left me there. I could have died."

Cooper stretched out his paw. "Uh, hello? Hero here."

"You are my hero, and I am so grateful for you. I should tell you that more often."

He coughed. "Oh, boy. Ms. Emotional is in the building."

I tapped his nose with my finger. "I guess I've realized I don't matter enough for him to stay here, and I'm okay with that. I promise. I wasn't exaggerating earlier. I'm at peace with it all."

"Ab," Cooper said.

"Oh, boy," Mr. Charming said. "Oh, boy."

"Cooper, you just ate," I said.

"That's not what I was going to say. I need to tell you something." He scooted closer to Bessie. "And you need to hear this too. The bird? He can leave."

"Oh, boy," Mr. Charming said. He flapped his wings and flew to his perch. "Remmington and Abby. Remmington and Abby."

"Now that the nuisance is gone," Cooper said. "Gabe was here. He came to see you the night I saved you."

"Stop playing around, Cooper."

"I'm not playing around. He was here."

"I don't appreciate—"

Bessie placed her hand on my arm. "He's not playing around. Let him finish."

"Thank you. He was here. He told you to let him go. You said you couldn't, but he said you had to for your own safety."

"Gabe knows I can take care of myself, and when I can't, I have you."

"He said something dangerous was happening. He didn't go into the details, but he cast a spell over you, Abby. To make you fall out of love with him. I don't know if he messed up or what, but you're being extra nice. It's weird."

I shook my head. "Now I know he's full of it."

"I'm not lying," Cooper said.

My shoulders stiffened. "Gabe would never do that to me."

"Things change."

I pressed my lips together and shook my head. "No. This is me. This is me falling out of love with him. Not some stupid spell." I poked my chest with my finger. "I changed how I feel. Me." My shoulders sank. "Are you being serious?"

He climbed onto my lap and stretched his front legs toward my neck. I picked him and held him in my arm.

"Okay," he said. "I guess we're getting close for this conversation. I'm being serious. I've never been more serious about anything in my nine lives. Well, eleven."

"I can fix this. I can create an undo spell."

"That's not what Gabe wants," Cooper said. "He didn't do this because he doesn't love you. It's the opposite. He loves you enough to force you to let him go. He wants to protect you. He believes allowing you to move on will keep you safe."

"Maybe it will but altering my feelings with magic doesn't mean those feelings don't exist. Everything will come crushing back once he removes the spell."

"If he intends to do that," he said.

A tear slid down my cheek. "You don't think he will? You don't think he's ever coming back, do you?"

"I don't know," he said.

"That's my point. He might. What happens then if I've moved on, moved on, like with someone else? If I've fallen for someone else? He returns, removes the spell and then what?" I stared at the card on the table. "I can't go with Remmington. I need to call him."

"No sweetie. Don't," Bessie said. "Go. You deserve to have fun, and I think you like Officer Sterling."

"I thought I did, but how do I know it's real? How do I know it's not Gabe's spell?"

"Gabe's spell isn't making you attracted to Remmington. It's allowing you to be open to the opportunity," Bessie said.

"But we don't know that for sure," I said.

"There's only one way to find out," Cooper said. He nuzzled his face into my neck. "Don't worry, Abs. I'll be there right by your side."

"Fine." I kissed the top of his forehead. "And once the festival's over, I'm going to find the mountain man and make sure he's out of Gabe's life forever."

WITCHY WONDERLAND

The Christmas season turns Holiday Hills into a magical, witchy wonderland filled with snowmen, sugar cookies by the dozen, and bottomless mugs overflowing with hot cocoa and whipped cream.

Everyone in town looks forward to the season, but all celebrating comes to a grinding halt when the big guy's messengers arrive with the worst of news.

It seems someone's stolen Santa's list and hidden it in Holiday Hills. Without it, Christmas won't happen, and a world without Christmas can never be the same.

But Abby and her familiar cat Cooper won't let that happen, not on their watch. Can they find the list and save the holiday?

WITCHY WONDERLAND IS a witchy holiday cozy mystery novella and is the sixth story in the Witches of Holiday Hills cozy mystery series.

Will Abby and Cooper save Christmas? Find out here.

ALSO BY CAROLYN RIDDER ASPENSON

The Rachel Ryder Thriller Series

Damaging Secrets

Hunted Girl

Overkill

Countdown

Body Count

Fatal Silence (Coming Soon!)

Deadly Means (Coming Soon!)

The Lily Sprayberry Cozy Mystery Series

Escrowbar Holder (Series prequel coming soon!)

Deal Gone Dead

Decluttered and Dead

Scarecrow Snuff Out Novella

Santa's Little Thief Novella

Signed, Sealed and Dead

Bidding War Break-In

Open House Heist

Realtor Rub Out

The Claus Killing Novella

Squatter's Fight Novella

Foreclosure Fatality

Upgraded for Murder

The Midlife in Castleberry Paranormal Cozy Mystery Series

Get Up and Ghost

Ghosts Are People Too

Praying For Peace

Ghost From the Grave

Deceased and Desist

Dèjá Bo

Haunting Hooligans: A Chantilly Adair Novella

The Pooch Party Cozy Mystery Series

Pooches, Pumpkins, and Poison

Hounds, Harvest, and Homicide

Dogs, Dinners, and Death

The Witches of Holiday Hills Cozy Mystery Series

There's a New Witch in Town

Witch This Way

Who's That Witch?

Another Witch Bites the Dust

Hungry Like the Witch

Witchy Wonderland (Coming Soon!)

The Midlife Psychic Medium Series

Formerly The Angela Panther Mystery Series

Unfinished Business

Unbreakable Bonds

Unbinding Love Novella

Uncharted Territory

The Ghosts Novella

The Christmas Elf Novella

Unexpected Outcomes

Undetermined Events Novella

The Event Novella

The Favor Novella

Undesirable Situations

Uncertain Circumstances

Untrue Accusations

The Garland Ghoul (Coming Soon!)

The Magical Real Estate Mystery Series

Spooks for Sale

A Haunted Offer

Other Books

Mourning Crisis

Join Carolyn's Newsletter List and receive special downloads, sales, and other exciting authory things here.

ABOUT THE AUTHOR

USA Today Bestselling Author Carolyn Ridder Aspenson writes cozy mysteries, thrillers, and paranormal women's fiction featuring strong female leads. Her stories shine through her dialogue, which readers have praised for being realistic and compelling.

Her first novel, Unfinished Business, was a five-star Reader's Favorite, a Rone Award finalist, and a number one bestseller on both Amazon and Barnes and Noble. In 2021, she introduced readers to detective Rachel Ryder in Damaging Secrets. Overkill, the third book in the Rachel Ryder series, was one of Thrillerfix's best thrillers of 2021.Reviews have praised her work as *'compelling, and intense,'* and *'read through the night, edge of your seat thrillers'*.

Prior to publishing, she worked as a journalist in the suburbs of Atlanta where her work appeared in multiple newspapers and magazines. She wrote a monthly featured column in Northside Woman magazine.

Writing is only one of Carolyn's passions. She is an avid dog lover and currently spoils two pit bull boxer mixes. She lives in the mountains of North Georgia as an empty nester with her husband, a cantankerous cat, and those two spoiled dogs. You can chat with Carolyn on Facebook at Carolyn Ridder Aspenson Books or through her website at www.carolynridderaspenson.com